A BUNCH OF MONKEY MALARKEY

AN AC SILLY CIRCUS CO. MYSTERY

WRITTEN BY ANN CHARLES

ILLUSTRATIONS BY C. S. KUNKLE

To Gigi the Bird.
You make my heart sing and want crackers!

A Bunch of Monkey Malarkey

Cover Art by C.S. Kunkle
Cover Design by B Biddles
Editing by Eilis Flynn
Formatting by B Biddles
Library of Congress: 2018911990
E-book ISBN-13: 978-1-940364-60-5
Print ISBN-13: 978-1-940364-59-9

Also by Ann Charles

AC Silly Circus Co. Mystery Series

Feral-LY Funny Freakshow (Novella 1)

Deadwood Mystery Series

Nearly Departed in Deadwood (Book 1)
Optical Delusions in Deadwood (Book 2)
Dead Case in Deadwood (Book 3)
Better Off Dead in Deadwood (Book 4)
An Ex to Grind in Deadwood (Book 5)
Meanwhile, Back in Deadwood (Book 6)
Wild Fright in Deadwood (Book 7)
Rattling the Heat in Deadwood (Book 8)
Gone Haunting in Deadwood (Book 9)
Don't Let it Snow in Deadwood (Book 10)

Deadwood Shorts: Seeing Trouble (Book 1.5)
Deadwood Shorts: Boot Points (Book 4.5)
Deadwood Shorts: Cold Flame (Book 6.5)
Deadwood Shorts: Tequila & Time (Book 8.5)

Jackrabbit Junction Mystery Series

Dance of the Winnebagos (Book 1)
Jackrabbit Junction Jitters (Book 2)
The Great Jackalope Stampede (Book 3)
The Rowdy Coyote Rumble (Book 4)
Jackrabbit Junction Short: The Wild Turkey Tango (Book 4.5)

Dig Site Mystery Series

Look What the Wind Blew In (Book 1)
Make No Bones About It (Book 2)

Goldwash Mystery Series (a future series)

The Old Man's Back in Town (Short Story)

Acknowledgments

Thank you to my husband for helping me come up with some funny freakshow adventures in Louisiana, one of our favorite states to visit.

Thanks to my two kids who laughed at my ideas for were-characters and reminded me of swamp critters we've seen during our travels.

Super-sized thanks to my editing crew—first-draft die-hards, Eilis Flynn (my amazing editor), and superstar beta readers. I appreciate you all helping on short notice yet again.

Thank you to my brother, CS Kunkle, for drawing the perfect freakshow characters for the cover and illustrations.

Thank you to all of my readers for coming along to enjoy a romp in this strange yet amusing circus world.

And thank you to my dad and uncle, aka the monkey brothers, for being such wonderfully entertaining role models.

Dear Reader,

You know how some parents claim one of their children was a surprise baby who wasn't planned? Often, it's the first or last child, who took it upon itself to come into this world "ready or not." Well, this AC Silly Circus Mystery Series is my version of a surprise baby.

I wrote the first novella, FERAL-LY FUNNY FREAKSHOW, after an invitation from an author friend to dabble in her universe. What came out with that first story was a whole new fun shapeshifter world that I loved, but I wasn't planning on writing a series in that new world. As most of you know, I have my hands full with my other "children" in the Deadwood, Jackrabbit, and Dig Site series worlds. I published that first novella and walked away, sorry to say good-bye to the characters but knowing I had to leave.

For eight months I played along in my usual sandbox, keeping my head down, trying not to think of Nora and Bruno and the crazy adventures in their circus freakshow world. Then came my "surprise"—the rights to that first novella were going to be returned to me in full. Nora and Bruno were mine again, along with all of their circus shapeshifting friends. The series ideas I'd played with while writing that first story (and kept pushing away because there was no future in it) came flooding back. The underlying seeds of possibilities for more funny circus adventures that my right brain had sprinkled on the pages sprouted.

Now, one year after the release of that first novella, I'm sharing with you my surprise baby—the second novella in the AC Silly Circus Mystery Series: *A BUNCH OF MONKEY MALARKEY*.

I hope you enjoy reading this newest wacky mystery with Nora, Bruno, and the rest of the circus freaks as much as I did writing it!

~ Ann

www.anncharles.com

FERAL FREAKSHOW
YOU
WON'T
BELIEVE
WHAT YOU SAW

Chapter One

Tippytoe, Louisiana
Madam Electra's Fortune Teller Tent
One hour until showtime

I'm thinking about taking up sword swallowing, Electra," said the bear of a man sitting across my parlor table from me.

"Sword swallowing?" My palms hovered over Ol' Blue, the crystal ball handed down through my family for generations. "Eugene, you just got over your fear of swallowing fire. Why do you want to mess with a good thing?"

Eugene had a popular act here at AC Silly Circus's freakshow division. He started out as "The Giant Man," making the crowd "oooh" and "ahhh" with his intimidating human size. Then he shapeshifted into his furry werebear self, lit the end of a torch on fire, and swallowed the flames, all without burning himself alive in the process.

"Fire is boring these days, not to mention the heartburn is a killer. You wouldn't believe how many antacid pills I've gone through already this week."

"That's because we're in Cajun country. You've been eating spicy jambalaya and garlic seafood gumbo since we hit the state line. Plus, all those deep-fried boudin balls you keep popping in your mouth like candy can't be helping your gut. I thought you were off pork, anyway." His doctor had recently told him that too much pork fat in his diet made him more flammable.

"Oh, those aren't the pork boudin. They're alligator with rice and peppers mixed in and deep fried to a crispy brown perfection." He licked his chops at the mention of them.

I grimaced. His stomach acid had to be nearing a Chernobyl meltdown. "And you want to stick a sword down into that fiery smelter you call a stomach?"

He shrugged. "I need to mix up my act a little. It's starting to feel like yesterday's news." He pointed a hairy-knuckled finger at Ol' Blue. "What does your magic ball say about my crowd tonight? Am I going to fill the seats?"

Fill the seats? I lowered my hands to the table on each side of my crystal ball. Eugene usually wasn't concerned about his show's attendance, more about his act going off without a hitch—or an inferno. It didn't take a psychic to figure out that something else was spurring this change for him.

"Eugene, why did you really come here today? And don't tell me it was for a prediction about the size of your crowd this evening, because I call bullshit on that. You've never cared about how many folks showed up before." I leaned closer, watching his round eyes and whiskered cheeks for telltale signs of lying. "Are the monkey brothers pressuring you into swallowing swords to bring in more money?"

Donatello and Marco, aka the monkey brothers, were middle-aged wereapes currently acting as the freakshow's co-ringmasters. Known throughout the circus world for their business acumen, they had built their stellar reputation on their food stand enterprise, which had grown more popular than the Mad Monkey magic act that they had debuted decades ago. However, since they'd been asked to stand in after the last ringmaster had an emotional breakdown, they'd been working on "improving" several others' freakshow acts for one reason or another. They claimed their intentions were to help the circus staff members up their games, but I saw through their smoke and mirrors. It was all about a healthy bottom line.

Eugene shifted in my parlor chair, scratching his hulking shoulder against the seatback. The wood creaked under his weight. "Well, Donatello might have suggested that if I doubled my crowd size, he could swing an assistant for me."

Of the two brothers, Donatello was the bigger penny-pincher. He was often seen rushing around the circus, howling out orders, while insisting he had no time to deal with whatever problem was at hand.

"Why do you need an assistant?" I asked.

Eugene's act was pretty basic. Like my fortune-teller routine, he'd been running his show on his own since he started in the circus business. Maybe he was getting lonely, though. I certainly had been until the head of security started sharing my bed every night.

Eugene held up his large right hand, stretching out his fingers. "The older I get, the harder it is to use lighters or strike matches with my big bear hands."

"You mean *bear* paws or *bare* paws." When he just frowned at me in response, I said, "Never mind. Aren't you wearing your special torch-glove during the show?" He'd had a special metal glove with a built-in torch made for his right paw to alleviate his grip problem.

"No. I kept burning myself with it." He held his left hand up for me to see. Sure enough, his knuckles were hair-free, singed clear to the skin. "Last night, I dropped two matches and ended up calling for a volunteer from the crowd to light the last torch."

"Crowd participation is a good thing." I tried to come at this with a positive attitude. Eugene had enough insecurities without Donatello picking apart his act.

He wrinkled his long nose. "Not when it comes to fire. Somehow word got to Donatello about what happened. He stopped by early this morning and read me the riot act. Apparently, a customer messing with fire is an insurance no-no. If anything happens and we have to file a claim, the insurance company will either triple our rates or drop us entirely."

I sighed. Of course, the almighty dollar played a role in all of this. Ever since the monkey brothers took over, we'd had what they called "troop scrums"—aka early-morning meetings from hell. During these bleary-eyed rallies under the big top, the brothers went from one shifter to the next, citing the current tasks on our individual project lists, demanding each of us report what we accomplished the night before. They didn't seem to understand that this circus was about so much more than productivity percentages and revenue streams; that there were living and breathing folks involved who had big hearts and fragile egos.

Damn. I missed the days when all I had to do was give psychic readings without worrying about my return-on-investment profitability ratio.

"And here I always thought bonobo apes were more interested in romance than financial gain," I muttered.

"The monkey brothers are only half bonobo on their mother's side. The other half is busybody chimpanzee blood."

Right. Someone had mentioned their mother was the idealist who'd given them their Italian names.

"I just wish I had an assistant," Eugene continued with slumped shoulders. "Someone to help me with my act each night and make sure my net profits exceed my next pen dentures."

His next what? Oh, wait. I grinned. "You mean *expenditures*."

He grunted. "Did I tell you that Donatello wants me to keep track of how many matches I go through each night? He's keeping an inventory list on his clipboard for all of us."

"Oh, jeez!" I crossed my arms. "What a bunch of monkey malarkey."

I could see now why an assistant appealed to Eugene. If the monkey brothers didn't back off, none of us were going to have time to practice our acts, let alone perform them. Maybe I needed to have a talk with Donatello to try to convince him to loosen up a little on the bookkeeping front. Not all of us lived and breathed debits and credits.

"Listen, Eugene," I started.

The sound of footfalls in my waiting room on the other side of my parlor's red velvet curtains made me pause. I could hear someone huffing. I sniffed, picking up a hint of cigar smoke.

"Madam Electra?" Marco, the taller of the two monkey brothers, called out from the other room. His voice was a notch higher than usual. "I need your help."

Eugene and I exchanged a raised-brow look. Normally, Marco and Donatello insisted on not being interrupted so close to showtime while they performed their last rehearsals alone in their tent. Why they would need my assistance at this point was beyond me.

I draped a velvet shroud edged with beads over Ol' Blue. My werecoyote instincts were skittish about letting the bean-counting businessman see my crystal ball for some reason. "Come in, Marco."

He rushed through the curtain, wearing his red and black ringmaster getup, magician's hat and all. His face was a roadmap of frown lines that doubled at the sight of Eugene sitting there. "I need you to come with me."

Eugene's eyes widened. "Me?" he croaked, sounding like a kid busted with his hand in the cookie jar.

"No, not you. I need Madam Electra."

"Why did you look at me when you said it, then?" he asked.

Marco growled. "It was an accident." He turned to me, his gaze intense. "Electra, could you please follow me to my tent?"

I stood, yet hesitated, wary. The anxiety rippling off of Marco was almost palpable. "What's going on?"

He shot a scowl toward Eugene. "I'd rather not discuss it in mixed company."

"I'm not mixed," Eugene said, his chin jutting. "I'm a purebred *Ursus arctos horribilis*, otherwise known as a North American brown bear to the science folks, but you can just call me a grizzly."

I did a double take. "If you're a purebred grizzly, what are you doing at a freakshow?"

Most of the shapeshifters who worked at this division of the circus were hybrids, mixed in a manner that made them freaks among the regular shapeshifting population. I had thought I was the exception, since I was a purebred werecoyote. Fortunately, my abilities as a psychic allowed me to blend with the rest of the circus folks, although it did take many of them some time to accept me due to my non-hybrid pedigree.

"My tail is a few inches longer than normal, my snout is fatter, and my ears are too pointy. My mother always claimed it was advanced engineering on her part, but short of a red glowing nose, I stick out like a bear version of Rudolph the Reindeer amongst my contemporaries."

Marco snorted. "Listen, we don't have time to discuss Eugene's lineage and genetic abominations."

"Abominations?" Eugene sat up tall. "That's hitting a little below the belt, apeman."

"I told you before, we're monkeys."

"I may be a bit slow in the morning and colder months, but even I know that chimps and bonobos are apes, not monkeys."

The monkey brothers shunned the A-word in public. According to rumor, their mother was a shapeshifting bonobo who'd been mated with a chimpanzee while locked away in some scientific laboratory. She'd escaped while pregnant, finding her way to the circus. When the babies were born, she'd insisted on calling them "monkeys" rather than "apes" in order to shield the fraternal twins from possible capture because she feared they'd be locked away and experimented upon for the rest of their lives. Their mother was long gone, but the brothers continued to use the "monkey" moniker out of fear of being caught and imprisoned.

"Fine, I take it back," Marco told Eugene and then turned to me again. "Come with me, please. We need to hurry. The show starts soon."

"Do I need any of my tools of the trade?"

"No." He glanced around my tent, his focus moving from the jeweled lamps, to the velvet- and silk-draped chests covered with various marketing fliers listing my services, to the smoke from my jasmine incense, to the padded chair I sat in behind my parlor table, before settling on Ol' Blue, which was still under wraps. "Maybe. I don't know."

Without another word, he raced out of the tent.

I followed empty-handed. Eugene lumbered along behind me.

We zigzagged through the red and white striped tents, rushing to keep up with Marco. He held open the flap of the large private tent he shared with his brother, leading us through a small sitting room with plush furniture to a side room where the walls were lined with what I figured were magicians' trunks. The back room wasn't nearly as lavish and smelled musty with a hint of cigar smoke.

"I need you both to promise you'll keep this a secret." He eyed us in turn.

Was this part of their magic act? Was Marco using us as test subjects? If so, it was working well. My heart was pounding while my legs were ready to pull a "coyote" and run.

I nodded. Eugene followed my lead.

Marco walked over to a red trunk standing on end with several small holes drilled into the lid. Two white rabbits were painted on the top. He unfastened the lid. It creaked open, giving me goose bumps. Marco stepped aside and held out his arm in a grand gesture to reveal what was waiting inside …

Which turned out to be his brother, Donatello, in his wereape form. His black magician ensemble lay in a wrinkled pile at the bottom of the trunk. Inside the box, Donatello sat on his haunches and stared at us with an empty expression.

I had a sudden urge to hand him a banana. What was this? Some kind of new thought manipulation the brothers were working on for the show?

"I don't get it." Eugene spoke first. "Is this part of your act?"

"No."

I frowned at Marco. "Then why are you keeping Donatello in this trunk?"

"I'm not. He's in there of his own will and he won't come out, not even when I try to force him." Marco pulled up his sleeve, showing us what appeared to be a bite mark on his wrist.

I looked back at the ape in the box. "I don't understand."

"Neither do I," Marco said. "That's why I need your help."

"Did he do a magic trick on himself?" Eugene asked.

"Maybe," Marco answered. "But since I can't get him to talk to me—or even use sign language—I have no idea."

"How long has he been in the trunk?" I asked.

Marco took off his hat and scratched his bristly flattop. "I don't know the answer to that, either. I was out at the front gate helping get things ready for our opening, and when I arrived back here a half hour ago to practice at our usual time, I couldn't find Donatello. I assumed he was running late doing his pre-show rounds, so I started setting up for the show. That's when I found him in the trunk where we keep the white rabbits we use in our show." He glanced around at the other trunks. "To add to the mystery, the rabbits are missing."

I stepped closer to Donatello, waving my hand in front of his eyes. He stared right through me, blinking every so often. "It's like some sort of trance."

"Maybe it's a curse of some sort," Eugene said, poking Donatello in the cheek several times and getting no response.

"Stop messing with him, Eugene." Marco put his hat back on and checked his watch. "What are we going to do? The show starts in under an hour. I can't work with him like this."

I rubbed my jaw, trying to think. The only sort of magic I'd heard of that could put a person in a trance was the dark sort. My grandmother, who had taught me all about being a seer, had told me to avoid dark magic at all costs. *The toll on a psychic's aura is too great*, she'd tell me when I pressed for more answers, warning me that sticking even a single toe in those waters risked being pulled in over my head.

"For now, we need to come up with a different opening act." I glanced around the tent, zeroing in on a pink trunk with kittens painted on the lid. "Marco, can you use Lemon Drop and Lolli Pop as your assistants and do enough of your magic act to appease the audience until the rest of us are set up and ready for our usual shows?"

Lemon and Lolli had been adopted by the monkey brothers years ago. The guys had taken them in when the two werecats had shown up after running away from an orphanage. Under the brothers' stern but loving hand, the two girls had grown into beautiful young women with a contortionist act that astounded all who attended their show. Their cats-in-boxes act sold out almost every night, especially to families with young children.

Marco puffed his round cheeks. "I guess so. The girls helped us when they were young." His eyes softened at the memory.

"Good. Eugene, go round up the girls."

Eugene lumbered off, leaving me alone with the two brothers.

"We need to let security know about this," I said, pointing at Donatello. "There might be foul play involved."

Marco's thick eyebrows wrinkled. "You think someone did this to Donatello on purpose?"

I shrugged. "It's possible. Magic works in different ways. In the wrong hands, it can be deadly."

"Yeah, but you're a sorceress."

"No, I'm a psychic."

"Close enough."

I swallowed a scoff. In what universe were those two close to the same? The panic in Marco's eyes kept my mouth shut. For now, I'd let him hold onto that thought if it gave him the hope he needed to get through the opening show.

"There has to be something you can do for him." Marco pressed, wringing his hands together.

Honestly, I wasn't sure where to start. I was accustomed to helping those who could talk and ask me and my crystal ball questions.

"Maybe." I wondered if Ol' Blue would be able to give me any hints on where to start with this mystery. "First, we need help from someone who's good at sniffing out crimes."

Marco groaned and dropped onto one of the trunks. "We

have to keep this quiet, Electra. If word gets out to the local police, they'll come and take Donatello away to a lab somewhere to poke and prod. He'd rather die than go through what Mother warned us would happen if that day ever came."

I squeezed his shoulder. "Nobody is taking anyone to a lab. I was talking about Bruno."

Head of the freakshow division's security, Bruno Maska was the ideal mixed breed to sniff out trouble and take down criminals. His mother had been a St. Bernard shifter and his father like me, a werecoyote. Their genes had blended to create the perfect law dog, both in the flesh and fur form. The big hunk was easy on the eyes, too, with those long dark eyelashes, brawny shoulders, and tight …

But I digress.

"Go get Bruno and bring him here," I ordered Marco, trying to snap him out of his sudden despondency. "Between the two of us, we'll figure out what's going on with Donatello and if someone else is behind this."

After one last frown in his brother's direction, Marco rushed out of the tent, leaving me alone with Donatello.

I returned to the rabbit trunk, studying the unresponsive ape. Why had he shapeshifted? Had someone forced him to change to his were-form? Or had it been self-inflicted? Or self-defense? Was he hiding from something when it happened? Or was he like Eugene, who shifted whenever his anxiety red-lined?

Once again, I waved my hand in front of the wereape's eyes.

Still no reaction. I took a deep breath, focusing outward, feeling through the dark with my mind. I had a strong notion that Donatello was stuck in his body somehow, unable to penetrate the wall blocking his conscious self.

"Who did this to you?" I asked. "Did you piss someone off with your nickel-and-diming? Or does this have to do with something else involving money? Did you double-cross someone you shouldn't have?"

I knew plenty from experience when it came to betraying a

criminal mind. My past screwup was the reason I was standing here trying to make a catatonic ape speak.

Donatello blinked, his expression remaining lost, unfocused.

My chest tightened as a thought flitted past. Had somebody come looking for me? Had they tried to get Donatello to talk and he'd resisted? Was his current state my fault?

My knees felt a little quivery all of a sudden. I moved to a trunk with the big top tent painted on it and sat. "Please, not again," I whispered.

After a moment, the wave of unease passed. My fault or not, I needed to work out what was wrong with Donatello before everyone else found out and started panicking again. After the fiasco we had at Tinkerville, the last thing this freakshow needed was another dead shapeshifter.

Chapter Two

I was still sitting on the big top trunk, practicing my tarot card memory exercises while I waited for Marco to return, when Bruno came striding into the monkey brothers' tent. He wore his black security T-shirt, faded blue jeans, and a cocky grin.

"Marco says I've been summoned by the great and mysterious Madam Electra," Bruno said. He'd taken to coming up with various monikers for me lately, especially after sex when he was lying next to me wearing nothing but a satisfied smile. When he took a closer look at my face, his grin slipped away. "What's going on?"

I stood and pointed at Donatello.

Bruno's gaze followed, his brow wrinkling. "There's a monkey in the box."

"Exactly."

He walked over to the trunk. "Shouldn't he be in a barrel?"

"Not funny," I said, even though it was, a little.

Marco joined us, his face glistening with perspiration.

"I don't get it," Bruno said, his gaze bouncing from me to Marco. "Is this part of your show opener?"

Marco crossed his arms, his scowl abrupt. "You've seen our act. It's far more sophisticated than a mere monkey in a trunk."

"My job is to watch customers, not the show." Bruno moved next to me. "To keep an eye out for troublemakers."

"Which is why I requested your presence here," I said. "Something's wrong with Donatello."

Bruno harrumphed. "I know. He keeps sticking his nose in places it doesn't belong, like the budget for my security team."

"What do you mean?" I asked, noticing Marco was avoiding Bruno's glare.

"Scrooge McMonkey over there in the box stopped by my office yesterday and wanted to take a look at our list of expenditures and inventory spreadsheets, asking all sorts of questions about our monthly budget allowance. I had to remind him that my security team doesn't fall under this division's umbrella."

"It doesn't?"

He shook his head. "We work for corporate—as in AC herself. Donatello and Marco have no jurisdiction when it comes to my department."

I frowned at Marco. "Has Donatello been going around to everyone in the circus and pestering them for inventory numbers and other accounting shit like that?"

The wereape's nod was slight. "We want to boost our profit margin and look good on paper for our next management meeting with AC."

Bruno growled, wrinkling his upper lip in Donatello's direction. I resisted the urge to bare my teeth and join him. The monkey brothers had been in charge a little over a week and they were already acting mad with power.

"You know what this means, Marco?" I asked. "If your brother is the victim of some sort of foul play, then everyone he's harassed about cutting costs and reporting numbers is a suspect."

Marco squeezed the bridge of his nose. "I told Donatello that we should focus our energy on building profits with marketing, but he insisted that tightening our belts would have a quicker effect without spending more money."

"I'm going to need a list of all of the staff members Donatello badgered lately," Bruno said, taking a wide-legged stance that came natural to the circus's top security dog.

Marco nodded. "But what are we going to do about my brother's condition? I can't keep him in that trunk all night."

"Maybe Bruno and you can carry him to his bed for now," I suggested. "As soon as we close the gates tonight, I'll return with Ol' Blue and see if I can find out anything more."

With a temporary plan in place, Bruno and Marco moved Donatello from the trunk. Lemon and Lolli arrived shortly after, wearing their matching contortionist cat suits, their faces tight with worry for Donatello. I tried to console the two petite girls, assuring them Bruno and I would dig into this after the show was over, but for now they needed to help Marco. As always with the circus, the show had to go on.

Bruno followed me out into the warm afternoon sunlight. As soon as we were out of earshot of Marco and his girls, I asked him, "How come you didn't mention anything last night about Donatello stopping by your office?"

"You were naked when I walked into your tent."

"First of all, it's *our* tent now," I reminded him. Our current living arrangement was agreed upon partly for my protection, but mainly because Bruno liked to frequent my bed and I didn't like him leaving it until the next morning. "Second, I wasn't naked."

He grinned. "Until you take some of that girly stuff off the walls, it's *your* tent. No testosterone-filled male would dare to lay claim to all of those veils and beads and sweet-smelling candles. And you were *too* naked."

"I was wearing a camisole and underwear, and you never seem to mind the veils and beads when I'm wearing them in *our* bed."

"That's different. I get to strip those off of you and play with what I find under all of that sexy packaging."

I rolled my eyes. "You're hopeless."

"When it comes to you, gorgeous, I'm a full-on catastrophe." He caught my hand as we neared my tent, pulling me to a stop. "I need to keep an eye on the front gate. How about you wait for me to wrap up and return here tonight before checking on

Donatello?"

"No way. You take too long."

"I'll make a point of hurrying."

I could tell by the intensity in his stare that this was more of a command than a request, but Bruno knew I tended to buck when he used vinegar instead of honey. "Why don't you want me over there without you?"

He shot a frown in the direction of the main gate, and then he took a step closer, lowering his voice. "What if this deal with Donatello is tied to your other situation, Nora?"

His use of my real name spoke of the gravity of the situation. I wasn't surprised that Bruno had jumped to the same suspicion I had regarding the contract out on my head. The real reason I was hiding behind my Madam Electra disguise was never far from his or my thoughts. Bruno's protection played a big role in why I was able to stay at the circus, pretending to be someone I wasn't, while hiding out from the bounty hunters after my skin.

Bruno being my fated mate as well as my protector was a bonus we both enjoyed, although I tended to fret about his future more often than not. Sometimes I used Ol' Blue on the sly to keep an eye on him. I knew Bruno would stand between a bullet and me in a heartbeat. The thought of losing him now that we'd found each other made it hard to breathe at times in the middle of the night when the worry demons were performing the Mexican Hat Dance on my chest.

"Okay," I conceded, squeezing his hand. "I'll wait for you to come to my tent before going over there."

"*Our* tent," he corrected with a small grin. He lifted my hand, brushing his lips over my knuckles. The warmth in his gaze made my pulse palpitate. "Don't forget to keep the stun gun within reach."

"It's strapped to the underside of my parlor table."

"What about the pocketknife I gave you?"

"It's tucked under the cushion on my chair."

One of his dark eyebrows rose. "The canisters of pepper

spray?"

"I put one next to the bed and the other in my chest of soothsayer accessories."

"And the brass knuckles?"

"They're in my underwear."

His eyes widened. "Are you serious?"

"Would I joke about brass in my panties?"

A smile spread slowly along his lips as he leaned closer. "Maybe we should go inside the tent so I can see for myself."

The radio attached to his belt squawked, followed by someone calling his name over the air.

"Save it for later, Romeo." I shoved him back a step. "The show's about to start and somebody just tugged on your leash."

He caught me by the shoulders and pulled me back, giving me a thorough kiss in spite of another crackle from his radio. "Be careful tonight, Madam Mayhem."

"Don't worry about me. Focus on Donatello."

He groaned, staring down at my cleavage. "I wish I didn't have to analyze anything other than the current state of you and your body."

"My body and I are still alive, thanks to you."

"You know what I mean."

I patted his chest. "Go to work, Bruno. I'll think of you every time the brass knuckles rub me the right way."

He cursed at the sky and then strode away without looking back. I enjoyed the view of his backside in those faded jeans until he slipped between two tents and disappeared.

Inside my parlor, I prepped for another afternoon and evening filled with telling fortunes and predicting love or heartbreak. Before long, my waiting room was filled with customers anxious to sit across from Ol' Blue and me.

It was nearing midnight by the time Bruno returned. I'd wrapped up with my last customer a half hour prior and sent the lovesick werewolf on her way with predictions of babies—many babies—in her near future with the alpha male she was currently dating. Although the crystal ball had shown me the alpha's brother, too, whose domineering nature she'd complained about incessantly while I tried to focus.

"You ready?" Bruno asked after stepping through the velvet curtain into my parlor. But a frown creased his face. His gaze moved from me to Ol' Blue as I settled it into the lockbox my grandmother had handed down to me along with the crystal ball. "Let me carry that for you."

I stepped back so he could take it, leading the way out of my tent. Bruno closed the flap behind us.

He was quiet as we walked, oddly so. "Did something happen at work tonight?" I asked.

He glanced my way. "No, why?"

"You seem troubled."

His gaze lowered to the ground. "I've been thinking about something."

When he didn't elaborate, I pressed. "Bruno, what's wrong?"

"I feel like I'm rushing you."

We weren't walking that fast. "You mean now? On our way to the monkey brothers' tent?"

"No, I mean with you and me—us. I'm rushing you into a relationship."

I stopped in my tracks and looked up at the sky. Was it a full moon? Nope.

Bruno looked back at me, slowing to a stop as well.

"Where is this coming from?" I asked. In my mind, I was thinking somewhere from the vicinity of planet Neptune.

"I told you, I was thinking about us."

"Why would you do that?" It wasn't like Bruno to think much beyond sex. Wait, that wasn't fair to him. His thoughts delved deeper than that in many ways, not to mention he was funny and caring, but still sex was up near the top most of the time.

"I don't want you to leave me," he explained.

"Why would I leave you?"

He came closer, lowering his voice. "Because I'm the one

who initiated our relationship and pushed you to exchange you-know-what."

We'd exchanged plenty of things since the first time we'd met—from insults to bodily fluids. "What in particular are you referring to?"

"The love bites."

It was actually more of a love nip that shapeshifters exchanged with their fated mates, sealing a monogamous deal between them. Sort of like vows, but with a deeper level that involved chemistry. Once we'd bitten each other, we were mated heart and soul, a fact that made me smile whenever I thought about it. I didn't know why he was having issues with this all of a sudden.

Officially, though, what Bruno said was true. He had pushed to bite me and make me his, however ... "Bruno, I told you before that I wanted you to do it. I was initially afraid of tying you to me because of my ugly past, but in my heart, I was already yours."

Instead of appearing to accept what I said and move on, the clouds storming over his features darkened even more. "I should have been more considerate of your feelings."

What in Hades was going on? Had I slipped into a parallel plane while toying with the spiritual realm tonight? I should have tethered myself more thoroughly. Or maybe it wasn't me. "Bruno, did you smoke some peyote tonight?"

He shook his head.

"Did you eat any funny-tasting brownies or cookies?"

"Huh-uh."

"Did somebody slip any pills into your coffee?"

"No. I made the pot of coffee myself."

I took his face in my hands, searching his gaze. His pupils seemed normal. Hmmm. "Did you hit your head?"

"No, Nora." His eyes grew moony. "I just couldn't stop thinking about you all night long."

Okay, this was really becoming kooky. "And normally you

don't think about me while you're at work, right?"

I wouldn't expect him to think about me. Bruno was the top security honcho because he was so good at his job. Before he'd recently returned to our freakshow family, he'd been promoted up the ranks to lead all of the AC Silly Circus Co.'s Security Department, reporting directly to AC herself. Then he came back to help solve the murder of one of our own beloved freakshow clowns, managed to break down the mental wall I'd built to keep him at bay, and transferred back to our little circus to watch over me and all of our friends.

A sheepish smile rounded his lips. "Well, I think about you naked off and on throughout the day."

For a moment good ol' Bruno was back, his gaze eating me up. "But not about our relationship?" I pressed.

In a blink, the worry lines returned to his face. He shook his head. "I'm sorry I rushed you, Nora."

I groaned and threw up my hands. "Bruno, you didn't rush me and now is certainly not the time for you to have a mental breakdown, so snap out of this bizarre brooding state and let's go see what's wrong with Donatello."

Without another word, he followed me through the maze of tents. His forehead was still creased when we reached the monkey brothers' tent.

What in the world was going on? Donatello was in some inexplicable trance-like state and now Bruno was acting like someone had pumped him full of teenager hormones.

"Hello?" I called as we stepped inside Marco and Donatello's tent.

"In back," Marco returned.

We found him in the side room with the magic trunks. Across the way, Marco was standing in front of the upright trunk his brother had occupied earlier.

"How's the patient?" I asked.

"See for yourself." Marco moved aside.

Donatello had returned to the trunk, sitting on his haunches and staring out at us with a blank look.

"Why is he back in the box?" Bruno asked.

"I don't know." Marco frowned at his brother. "He was here when I returned after the big top show, as if we'd never moved him."

I glanced around the room. Several of the trunks had been shifted, probably used in the magic act. "Where are Lemon and Lolli?"

"They went to their tent to get some rest. The extra show wore them out."

"Bruno, will you please pull one of those trunks over here and set my case down on it?"

After he did as I'd asked, he stepped back into the shadows to watch and wait. Bruno knew that I needed space to "see" what others couldn't.

I opened the case and pulled out Ol' Blue along with its stand. "Marco, do you have a chair I can use? Something comfortable would be best." Creaky, hard chairs made it tough to focus sometimes.

I could sit on the ground, which was soft enough, but I'd rather be able to look down on the crystal ball rather than up at it. I'd learned long ago that different views led to different visions, and staring down often resulted in a clearer picture of the past. Not that Ol' Blue ever spelled out answers to exactly what I asked. Instead, it tended to give me hazy ideas and clues. That's where my seer training and years of experience came into play.

Marco hauled in one of the lavish armchairs from their front room. The cushions smelled like Lolli's favorite cotton candy–scented perfume when I sat in it.

"Do you have some candles handy?"

He opened a trunk next to where Bruno stood watching me and pulled out several white candles already set in holders. I selected two and placed them on each end of the trunk I was using as a table.

I scooted to the front edge of the chair and ran my fingers over the crystal ball. Smooth and cool to the touch, Ol' Blue glowed to life as I tickled it awake the way my grandmother had taught me so long ago under the starry desert sky.

I stared across the ball at the ape in the box, seeing Ol' Blue's reflection in his dark pupils. "Okay, Donatello. Let's see if I can find out about what you've been up to and why you're so fond of that damned trunk."

Chapter Three

Long, long ago when I was a girl, my grandmother taught me a very important lesson about summoning and disturbing forces from another plane of existence. Without proper preparations and protections, these forces could attack and drain me, damaging my inner peace permanently, leaving me a broken vessel. She showed me several ways to build a force field around me and those nearby, and stressed the importance of taking the time to perform the appropriate rituals before seeking answers.

Fortunately, I'd already performed most of these routine rituals earlier in my tent. However, to be safe, I did take a moment to meditate and add one more protection to remove any chance of harm coming to Bruno, Marco, or Donatello.

I closed my eyes and took several deep breaths, seeking the zone of clearest sight within me. It took more effort without my sage incense. The weariness that came after hours of being "on" with customers didn't help either, but I'd been working with Ol' Blue for a long time. We rode the spiritual airwaves like a lone rider on her favorite horse.

"What say you, friend?" I whispered and massaged the cool glass for several seconds. Then I pulled my fingers away and opened my eyes. The crystal ball swirled with gray clouds. "Hmmm."

Marco tiptoed closer. "Is that bad?"

"It's not good. Gray usually means misfortune is at play."

I leaned over the ball, allowing my gaze to become unfocused as I looked into the churning shades of gray. "Show me what has caused the malady within this ape."

"Monkey," Marco corrected.

"Ape," I repeated with more emphasis, squinting at him for a moment. "The crystal ball is no fool."

He pinched his lips shut.

Again, I stared into Ol' Blue, my vision blurring for a moment before sharpening on what the ball was showing me.

An image took shape slowly, starting with two legs. Then I realized they weren't legs, but rather ears. Rabbit ears. Correction, make that long jackrabbit ears.

Finn!

One of the longer-running acts here at the freakshow was performed by Finn the Jackrabbit, a shapeshifter who preferred his furrier facade to his human one. Finn's act consisted of reading from a book full of Bugs Bunny quotes while speaking in various accents, his Scottish brogue being one of my favorites. Finn sold out his show every night, since his act was well known and loved by children and adults alike.

But what did Finn have to do with Donatello's current catatonic state? Was the jackrabbit shifter okay? Had he suffered some sort of misfortune unbeknownst to the rest of us? Finn was superstitious most days, using all sorts of tricks to avoid bad luck.

I covered a yawn, struggling for a moment to stay on task.

The smoky swirls inside the crystal ball grew more frenzied and took on an orange hue.

"Why is it turning orange?" Marco asked, peering over my shoulder.

"Orange usually speaks of some sort of hidden aggression or anger and other troubled emotions."

Was Ol' Blue telling me that Finn had some hidden aggressions? Or was this about Donatello?

As I continued to interpret what the ball was telling me, another image began to form in the clouds. I watched, focusing my inner eye, opening my mind to the forces within.

A blurry image of Bruno's face appeared, slowly taking a more defined shape. His brow was lined with concentration or worry … or both. My heart pounded in my throat. What did Bruno have to do with all of this? Was Ol' Blue picking up some residual thoughts about my conversation with Bruno on our way here, or was this something else?

"Oh no," Marco gasped. "It's turning red. Red is never good, is it?"

"Ol' Blue is warning me," I explained.

"Warning about what? Is something else going to happen to Donatello? Is he going to die in that trunk?"

"I don't know yet. Give me a moment to see." When Marco continued to hover, huffing in my ear, I said, "Bruno, help me out here."

Bruno stepped forward and took hold of Marco, pulling him away, giving me the space I needed.

After regaining my tranquility, I said, "Now, where were we?"

Through eddies of smoke, I saw a clear image of Donatello, only he was in his human form, not his current ape state. He was staring down at something. It took me several beats to figure out what the item was in his hands—his clipboard.

The ball reverted to its starting blue glow, the image inside fading, the swirls evaporating. The door to the other plane was closed. Apparently, that was all of the information I was going to receive.

"Why is it blue again?" Marco asked.

"This session is finished." I sat back and stretched my neck, drained physically as well as mentally. "I'm too tired to continue," I added, pushing away thoughts about how soft my pillow would feel right then. "We'll have to use what I learned for now and see where it leads us."

"Thank you," I told Ol' Blue and covered it with the velvet shroud. Sinking into the chair, I recited the closing chant that my grandmother had taught me would seal the door to the other plane until I needed to open it again.

"Well?" Marco asked, standing beside my chair. "What do we do now, Electra?" I could hear the tension in his voice. "How do we get Donatello to come out of that trunk and stay out?"

I stared at Donatello while massaging the back of my neck. I had an idea, but it was more of a search mission than anything to do with actually rescuing Donatello from his trunk. "We're going to go see Finn."

"Finn?" Marco scoffed. "That damned jackrabbit is probably high as a balloon by now. You know he decompresses with a joint after his show."

It wasn't only after his show that Finn found mind-altering ways to relax, but that was the jackrabbit's business, not Marco's.

I pushed to my feet. "High or not, I need to ask him a couple of questions." I looked over at Bruno. "You want to tag along?"

"Of course." He took Ol' Blue's lockbox from me after I put the crystal ball away.

Marco opted to stay back at the tent and keep an eye on his brother while Bruno and I headed for Finn's tent. We saw Eugene coming toward us across the grassy midway in striped pajama pants, a holey T-shirt, and hiking boots. Trailing behind him were two raccoons. At first I thought they were merely heading in the same direction as he was, but when Eugene stopped as we drew near, one of them climbed his leg. Its back foot caught in his bootlace, untying it as it yanked its foot free, and then clung to his knee like an opossum.

"What's with the raccoons?" I asked him.

"Are they friends of yours?" Bruno reached down to pet the bigger one that was near Eugene's ankle. It snarled up at him, adding a hiss for good measure after he yanked his hand back.

"I don't know." Eugene winced and extracted the raccoon clinging to his knee, setting it back on the ground. "They showed up midway through my show and joined me on stage. The crowd loved them, so I went with it. I figured Marco must have sent them to help me out so that I wouldn't have to ask someone in the crowd to light my matches."

"These two raccoons can light your flaming torch for you?" I watched as the smaller one Eugene had set down started to tie the big guy's hiking boot for him, its fingers deft.

"Yep." He sounded like a proud father. "I only had to show them once how to use the lighter Finn let me borrow. They picked up on the trick pretty quick. They're smart li'l buggers."

"Ornery, too." Bruno was still glaring at the raccoon that had hissed at him. "Are they shifters?"

"No, but they must have been someone's pets. They're too obedient to be feral."

The raccoon finished tying his boot and chattered up at him.

Something was odd about these two raccoons. They were acting more like doting aunts than regular animals, yet they didn't show any of the characteristics of shapeshifters. I leaned down and sniffed in their direction, smelling a musty forest-like scent coming from them. Nor did they smell like shifters.

"They weren't afraid of you when you were in your werebear form?" I asked.

"Not at all," Eugene said and scooped up the bigger one, cuddling it against his chest. "It was as if they knew I'd never hurt them." He scratched the raccoon behind the ears. "Isn't that right, li'l buddy?"

The raccoon purred.

"Hmmm," I said.

It seemed to be a sound I was making more and more lately.

Bruno looked over at me. "What's that for?"

I shook my head. "Nothing. Let's go find Finn. See you later, Eugene."

With a wave, the man-bear lumbered off with his two new friends, the smaller one waddling behind him to keep up.

I turned to Bruno. "Did anything about that scene seem odd to you?"

"Yes." He scratched his stubble-covered jaw, staring after the threesome. "That big raccoon growled at me."

"So?" Had Bruno noticed a sign of some nefarious force at work in the raccoon?

"Why do you think it did that?" he asked. "It didn't growl at you. Did it feel more threatened by me because I'm bigger than you? Or did it have to do with my voice being more baritone? Wait, it can't be either of those because Eugene is larger than me with a much deeper voice."

I crossed my arms. "What are you doing?"

"Trying to figure out what I did to that raccoon to deserve a growl. I thought I was being friendly."

"Seriously, Bruno, what is going on in your head tonight? You don't usually—make that *ever*—question things like our relationship or some other animal's ambiguous aggression."

He scrubbed his hand down his face. "I don't know. My brain keeps getting stuck on things tonight."

I grinned. "You certainly have a way with words."

He gave me a mock glare. "Keep it up, wench, and I'll throw you over my shoulder, take you back to our tent, and have my way with you."

"Is that a threat?"

"Yes." His brow wrinkled. "Or was that too strong? Did you feel overly threatened? Because I was just kidding. I wouldn't throw you over my shoulder unless you were okay with that. And I'd never force you to—"

"Bruno, shut up." I tapped my index finger on his forehead. "I think you have a wire loose up here."

He grimaced. "You think it's a tumor? I've heard if you start smelling burning hair it means—"

"Please stop before my ears start crying." I turned and walked away, heading for Finn's tent.

Bruno caught up with me outside the jackrabbit's tent flap. "Sorry about that back there," he said, sounding back to his old self. "I've had the weirdest day."

"You and Donatello, huh?"

"Yeah. I'm not usually so prone to self-analysis. I blame you."

"What?" I gaped at him. "Why me?"

"Because you're a saucy, seductive siren and before you got into my head, I never had this problem." His teasing grin took the bite out of his words. "So, why are we paying a visit to Finn so late?"

"I saw him in Ol' Blue through the gray swirls of misfortune. I want to find out if he is suffering from ill luck, or if this Donatello situation is somehow connected to him."

"What else did you see in your magic ball?"

I scowled at his description of Ol' Blue. "How many times do I have to tell you it's not a 'magic ball'?"

"Fine. Your all-seeing eye. Is that better?"

"A little," I conceded. I leaned in close to his ear. "I saw you in the orange."

"The orange? That's the warning one, right?"

"No, it's aggression or troubled emotions."

He grimaced. "Well, I've certainly been a hot emotional mess tonight."

"Yeah. It must be your time of the month."

He burst out laughing before I could cover his mouth with my hand.

"Hey, dude and dudette." Finn poked his head out through his tent flap. One of his long ears was listing to the side. He let out a puff of sweet-smelling smoke. "Did you come to have a little late-night roll and smoke with me?"

"No, I need to talk to you about something," I told him. "Can we come inside?"

"Uh …" He glanced over his shoulder. "My place is sort of messy. How about we talk out here?" He stepped outside with us, pulling the tent flap closed behind him.

Bruno and I exchanged glances of suspicion. Something was up with Finn. He usually didn't care how clean his tent was when I came to visit. Heck, I'd been in there amongst dirty clothes, stacks of books, and carrot butts littering the floor and furniture.

"What are you hiding in your tent, Finn?" Bruno asked,

getting straight to the point.

Oh, yeah, he was definitely back to normal at the moment.

"Nothing, man." Finn thumped his back leg a few times, his whiskers twitching as he avoided Bruno's stare by focusing on the smoking joint in his paw. "I just sort of let loose after my performance tonight and don't want anyone to see my sty."

I leaned closer and sniffed his black velour vest. "What's that smell?"

"It's Cajun peyote."

"No, not that." I sniffed again. Scents were like addresses for me, giving a range of details that pinpointed their source. "I smell the monkey brothers' tent."

He gaped at me. "You can smell that?"

"I'm a werecoyote, Finn. You know my sense of smell is one of my strengths." Along with my hearing. I plucked a white hair off his vest. "What's this?" Finn's was light brown, not white.

"What?"

"This white hair?"

He shrugged. "I'm getting old. My white hairs are coming in."

I held the hair under my nose, pretending to smell it. "This isn't yours."

"There's no fucking way you can pinpoint a rabbit by a single hair," he said, calling my bluff.

He was right. I couldn't, but he was high enough that I could pull the wool over his eyes. Normally, I wouldn't try mind games like that on him, but with Donatello in his trance and Ol' Blue linking it to Finn, I needed to know what the jackrabbit was hiding for his own safety.

I sniffed it again for show, and then I handed it to Bruno. "Bag that for evidence."

"Evidence for what?" Finn asked, his voice rising. "I'm clean, man!"

"Calm down, Finn," Bruno said, holding the white hair between his fingertips. "We're not here to arrest you, we just need your help."

"Crikey! I've nothing for ya, mates." He slipped into his Australian accent, trying to play it cool.

"I saw you in my crystal ball tonight, Finn," I explained.

The jackrabbit crossed himself, then fluttered his paws through the air between us, and followed that with some weird scissor move with his paw.

"What color was the smoke?" he asked me when he'd finished with his ritual.

"Gray."

"Oh, shit." He twitched his whiskers at Bruno. "Gray can't be good, can it?"

Bruno shook his head. "Nora says it means you've come upon some kind of misfortune. What we need to know is if that has something to do with what you're hiding in your tent."

"I'm not hiding anything."

I sighed, too tired for this crap. "Finn, we have a problem. Donatello is in some kind of trance and Ol' Blue linked him to you. Why?"

Finn thumped his other back leg on the ground. He started to say something and then brushed off the front of his vest.

"I'm worried you're in some kind of danger," I added. "And Bruno and I can't help you unless you tell me what's going on in your tent."

He took a hit off his joint, his eyes darting back and forth between us as he blew out the smoke. "Okay. If I come clean to you two, do you promise not to tell the monkey brothers what's in my tent?"

I hesitated. If it pertained to the situation with Donatello, then I might need to spill the beans. On the other hand, Finn was putting his trust in Bruno and me, and Finn was a good friend while the monkey brothers were my bosses.

"I promise, Finn." When Bruno didn't also give his word, I jabbed him in the stomach. "Come on, Bruno."

"Fine. I promise."

Finn nodded and disappeared inside of his tent. I heard a

creaking sound, and then he held the flap open for us. "Come in," he whispered, glancing to the left and right around us.

Bruno led the way. Inside, the place was actually clean, not a single carrot butt to be found. I scanned his small chairs and miniature cupboards, noting the neat stacks of books and a lack of peyote and cannabis paraphernalia. "What's the big deal?" I asked. "Everything looks clean as can be."

From out of his vest, Finn pulled a round, white hairy ball. "This is the big deal." He held it out toward me.

The tiny white bunny twitched its nose at me. "Is that … ?" I trailed off, hearing a thump come from the closed-up cupboard across the room. Bruno strode over and opened it. The cupboard door made the same creaking sound I'd heard while we were waiting outside. Sitting on one of the shelves was another white bunny. It gnawed on a piece of carrot, looking as cute and cuddly as the one in Finn's paws.

These two were the escapees from the rabbit trunk that Donatello was currently making his home. How had Finn come to have them?

"What are you doing with the monkey brothers' rabbits?" Bruno asked. I could tell by his expression that he was wondering if Finn had a hand in causing Donatello's catatonic state.

"They hopped up to me earlier while I was doing my pre-show sunbathing."

"Why didn't you take them back?" I reached out and stroked the tiny bunny's soft white fur.

"Because they deserve their freedom." Finn smiled down at the pudgy bunny, obviously smitten. "I'm searching for a good home for them, but it's not easy down here in Louisiana. I'm afraid they might end up mixed into a pot of gumbo."

Bruno smirked. "So, you're running some sort of underground bunny railroad now?"

"Maybe I am. They must have escaped for a reason."

"Finn." I tried to reason with him. "You know that Marco

and Donatello are good to their animals. Besides, they worked hard to train those rabbits for their act. They even went so far as to teach them to … Hey, is this one actually purring?"

Finn nodded. "But bunnies don't purr in their throat like cats, they rub their teeth together to make the sound."

"No kidding." I scratched it between its ears. "The monkey brothers are going to want these two cuties back, you know."

"I might be willing to give these kits back if the brothers are interested in making a deal."

"What sort of deal?" Bruno asked, closing the cupboard door with the bunny safely inside.

"Those money-grubbers can have their bunnies if Donatello stops pressuring me to shorten my show and start putting on two performances a night to double the revenue."

Chapter Four

Bruno and I left Finn to his bunny fun.

"You know what this new piece of information from Finn means, right?" Bruno asked.

Yeah, I did, but instead I said, "That you want a pet bunny."

He chuckled. "No, thanks. I have my hands full with a werecoyote who likes to use her cryptic crystal ball to meddle in everyone else's business."

I linked my arm in his, smiling up at the moon. " 'Meddle,' you say? You wound me, dear skeptic, with that sharp tongue of yours."

"Good." He grinned at me. "Then I can lick you better."

We walked a while in silence, stopping in front of the monkey brothers' tent.

"Should we go in and tell Marco how many suspects Donatello has made with his micro-managing?" I asked. It appeared nobody had escaped his clipboard and penny-pinching attempts, which meant that each and every one of us could be the villain who caused Donatello's predicament.

"No. You're tired."

I wasn't going to argue with him about that. "I am."

"Let's get you back to our tent and into bed."

I didn't argue about that either.

As we weaved through the tents toward ours, my arm still linked with his, Bruno told me, "I need to check out the monkey brothers' office first thing tomorrow morning."

"You don't want to do it tonight?"

"I'm not going to leave you alone. While the chances seem slim that what happened to Donatello has anything to do with your past coming back to *hunt* you, I don't want to take a chance."

I yawned, leaning my head on his shoulder. "Be honest. You just want to get me naked."

"Always. But not tonight. You probably don't want me pawing you after a long day."

Pawing me? What the hell? He was always considerate in bed, feeding my needs before his. "Who are you and what have you done with the real Bruno?"

"I just don't want to be one of those guys who—"

I pulled up short. "You're doing it again."

"Doing what?"

"Over-analyzing our relationship. What's going on with you?"

He frowned down at me. "I can't explain it. I keep feeling uncertain about everything, especially us."

"But why? I haven't given you any reason to feel insecure, have I?"

"No."

"This makes no sense. I'd blame the moon, but it's not even full."

We continued through the darkness, walking in silence.

At our tent, he tied the flap closed behind us and led me to our bed. I stripped down and crawled between the sheets, sighing as my head hit the pillow. "Tomorrow morning," I said, pausing to yawn, "I'll try Ol' Blue again. See if anything has changed with Donatello."

The bed shifted, his body warm as he pulled me close. "Tomorrow, we'll figure this out together. Now get some sleep, oh great Mesmerizing Madam Electra."

"I like when you use 'majestic' more."

"I know, but I thought we were talking about you."

I fell asleep with a smile on my face and dreamed I was stuck in the trunk next to Donatello, wishing I could escape the invisible bonds holding me there.

* * *

I woke just before sunrise, as I did every morning, so that I could go out and greet the sun with the chant my grandmother taught me many, many moons ago. I may no longer live amongst my people in the southwest desert, but I still followed their ways.

Bruno was awake when I came back inside feeling refreshed and playful from the sun's glowing start to the day. "Did you come up with an answer to our monkey problem?" he asked as I crawled back between the sheets next to him.

"Not yet." I snuggled up against his side, trailing my fingers over his chest. "But I have an idea about how we could go about brainstorming it."

"I'm all ears."

My hand slid southward, circling his navel before landing on more interesting terrain. "Really? Because this doesn't feel like an ear at all." I slid my fingers under the waistband of his briefs and took him in hand.

His eyes darkened as I stroked him awake. "Crawl on top of me, woman," he ordered a short time later, his voice guttural with need.

I did as ordered, my clothes getting in the way as he moved under me, rousing my body to match his.

"Let me inside," he said, his hips arching under me.

I disobeyed, egging him on further with an erotic hip-swaying dance that involved rubbing in all of the right places.

"Nora," he panted, his eyes dark pools. "You are so giving."

I was what? My movements stuttered, but then I continued, feeling more conscious and awkward. That was kind of a weird thing to say. Shaking it off, I leaned over and licked a trail down the side of his neck.

He groaned and took me by the hips, grinding harder.

"You like that?" I whispered.

He frowned at me. "Only if you feel comfortable doing it."

I stilled. "Comfortable?"

"I don't want you to feel like I'm rushing you into anything."

Rushing me into … "You've got to be kidding me." I sat up, straddling him. "Bruno, are you analyzing sex right now?"

"Well, officially it's not sex yet. This is only foreplay, which I am finding extremely pleasurable, but I don't want you to feel like you have to lick me if it's not something that you enjoy doing."

I scoffed. "Trust me, I like to lick you. All over." I reached out and ran my index fingernail down his sternum. "Now, would you like me to lick you somewhere else?"

His forehead lined. The seconds ticked and ticked.

"Bruno!"

"What? I'm weighing my answer."

"In case you didn't hear me right, I just offered to lick you in the most intimate way."

"I did hear you." He laced his fingers behind his head. "I was trying to decide if you really mean that, or if you're just saying it because you think I want you to lick me but you don't really take pleasure in exchanging oral foreplay."

My mouth fell open. "This is bananas. And you're nuts."

"Yeah." His gaze drifted sideways. "That's what scares me. I think I'm losing my mind. I can't stop focusing on how you feel about every move you and I make."

I sighed. "Normally, I'd say being concerned about my physical happiness is a good thing, but right now, I want you to get out of this head." I pointed at his noggin. "And into the other one." I rocked against him to be clear.

"I'll try."

I leaned down and kissed him the way he liked, hard and on the edge of frenzied. When I pulled back, I whispered, "Are you ready now?" He certainly felt more than ready.

He glanced at my mouth. "Did I hurt you with that kiss? I got a tad rough toward the end. I probably shouldn't have—"

"Oh, sweet hell! That's it." I rolled off of him and stood up. "Get dressed, nutter. Let's go figure out what's up with that ape."

He scowled, sitting up. "But I don't think we're done here."

"Trust me, until you can stop worrying about my feelings during sex, we're done. I'm not going to let you ruin our romantic life with over-analysis. I'm afraid I'll have an orgasm and you'll want to stop and talk about how *that* made me feel."

He groaned. "What is wrong with me?"

"I don't know," I said, sliding a star-covered mini-dress over my head. "But something tells me it's tied to this whole monkey mess going on right now because everything started going haywire for you and Donatello yesterday." I pulled my hair back in a ponytail. "Get your pants on, Dr. Sigmund Freud. We have a mystery to solve so that your raging, moral super-ego will shut up and let your sexy, primitive id return to take over in the sack."

Fifteen minutes later, Bruno and I were heading back to the monkey brothers' tent. We detoured to their food stand on the way to get some coffee. Eugene was standing at the order window when we arrived. At his feet were his two raccoon friends along with a skunk I hadn't seen before.

"Hey, Eugene," I said, stopping several feet away. I didn't trust skunks. They were often moody and too willing to lift their tail at a stranger. "Odd to see you so early in the morning."

The werebear tended to sleep in late every day, making sure he got at least eleven hours of sleep in lieu of hibernating for half of the year.

"Mr. Jingles woke me up."

"Who's Mr. Jingles?" Bruno asked.

The big guy pointed at the skunk that was currently standing on its back legs while pulling small threads off of Eugene's cutoff shorts.

"Is he a wereskunk?" He didn't look like one, or smell like it either, but this was the freakshow division of a circus, so I could be wrong.

"No, he's just very attentive. I found him in my tent this morning when I woke up." He reached down and patted Mr. Jingles on the head. "Thanks, buddy."

"What was he doing in your tent?" Bruno asked, giving the big raccoon the evil eye.

"Cleaning my bookshelf."

Eugene liked to read in his spare time. Erotic romances were his favorites, followed by gritty westerns.

"What do you mean, 'cleaning'?" Bruno asked. "If he's not a shapeshifter, how was he managing that?"

Eugene handed the skunk a piece of what looked like an egg and cheese po'boy sandwich. "He was using his tail as a duster. When he finished that, he laid out my clothes for me."

Bruno and I swapped a wrinkled brow.

Before we had a chance to question the bear shifter further, a red-colored squirrel came scampering up and raced past us, climbing Eugene's leg. He crammed something into the pocket of the big guy's shorts and then hopped down and took off across the grass again.

"What was that?" I asked.

"Oh, that's Fred," Eugene said.

"Fred who?" Bruno asked, still staring after the squirrel.

"Fred the fox squirrel. He just showed up about an hour ago and started stuffing my pockets with nuts." Eugene lifted his shirt to show us his bulging shorts pockets. He reached in and pulled out a handful of peanuts. "I don't know where he came from or who told him I was hungry, but the little guy won't stop. I've already emptied my pockets twice." He offered a handful to Bruno.

"He must be getting them from the elephants' tent," Bruno said, cracking open a peanut shell. "You say the skunk and squirrel just showed up?" At Eugene's nod, he continued, "Same as how the raccoons arrived unannounced last night?"

As if knowing they were the subjects of discussion, the two raccoons looked up at Bruno. The bigger one raised its upper lip. Apparently, it remembered their brief standoff and its heart hadn't grown any fonder for my fated mate. I crossed my fingers that Bruno wouldn't need another therapy session because of the damned raccoon's residual aggression.

"That's right," Eugene confirmed. "Donatello must have hired some help for me before he got that case of the jack-in-the-box disease."

Wait a second. First Donatello went to a statue state then Bruno started analyzing his feelings, and then Eugene gained a bunch of new pets. This seemed like the work of something more mischievous rather than evil. Had someone conjured an imp and set it free? Or could it be some sort of naughty fairy at work? Then again, we were in southern Louisiana, so maybe it was some sort of voodoo bugaboo.

Eugene stepped off to the side, waving his entourage to join him so that Bruno could place our coffee order.

"Did you figure out what's going on with Donatello?" he asked me.

I shook my head. "We're on our way over there right now to investigate further."

He broke the last of his po'boy in three pieces and handed them to his new friends. "Have you seen Hank this morning?"

Hank was in charge of the large animals at the freakshow. He was a weregorilla who looked almost the same when he was an ape or a human with his big flat nose, deep sunken eyes, and sloping forehead—especially when I was drunk. Of course, the black hair covering most of his body didn't help either. Hank had tried waxing his back and chest once. His howls of pain were heard throughout the circus.

"Not yet. Why?"

"I stopped by on my way here. His back is covered in scratches."

How could Eugene have seen them through all of that hair?

"What happened?"

"It's the weirdest thing. He said when he woke up this morning, Leon was in bed with him."

"Leon?" I snorted. "You mean *our* Leon?"

Leon was a werelion, the biggest shapeshifting feline in our division. He was known for his deep throaty voice, his extravagant taste in large belt buckles, and his gorgeous girlfriends … and boyfriends. Rumor had it that the king of the jungle was into wild sex, and he had no problem finding partners, which made me wonder why in the world he'd climbed into Hank's bed. Hank was nothing like the sleek sexy mates Leon typically favored.

"Yeah, that Leon." Eugene popped a couple of peanuts in his mouth, shell and all. "Hank said when he woke up, Leon was naked and spooning him, purring like crazy and kneading his back with his long, sharp fingernails. That's how he got the scratches."

I grimaced. "Oh, dear. I thought Hank preferred females, especially blondes." The ape shifter had a vintage poster of the original King Kong movie with a wilted Fay Wray in Kong's hand that he kept hung on his tent wall.

"Well, Leon is a sandy-haired blond officially," Eugene said, frowning as Fred the squirrel bounded back up his leg and stuffed another peanut in his pocket.

I watched the squirrel take off again across the grass. "Did Leon give any explanation as to why he was in Hank's bed?"

"Did you just say that Leon was in Hank's bed?" Bruno asked, handing me a steaming cup of coffee.

The big raccoon at Eugene's feet growled up at Bruno, earning a snarl in return.

After a nod at Bruno, I turned back to Eugene. "Well?"

"Leon was as flabbergasted by it as Hank. He swears he wasn't drinking last night, either. They both came to the conclusion that Leon sleepwalked and ended up in Hank's tent. Besides the scratches, neither of them remembers any hanky-panky going on."

"Hmmm." I took a sip of coffee, picking up hints of chicory.

"There's that 'hmmm' again," Bruno said, holding out a powdered sugar–coated beignet for me.

"Yeah." I took a bite of the beignet, which was still warm from the fryer. For a couple of seconds, I forgot all about amorous lions and blond-loving apes. "Mmmmm, that's better than sex."

"What's that supposed to mean?" Bruno asked, his cheeks darkening.

Oh, great Zeus's ass! Now the silly man was going to spend the morning beating himself up about that damned comment. "Drop it, Bruno." I shoved the rest of the beignet in my mouth.

"If you're referring to this mor—"

I held up my sugar-coated fingers, playing traffic cop. "Let's go see Marco."

We said our good-byes to Eugene and his entourage and headed toward the monkey brothers' tent in silence. Bruno brooded as we walked, while I cursed whatever force it was that had turned my normally bold alpha male into a self-doubting worrywart.

One way or another, I was going to get to the bottom of this mess before Bruno drove me to drink.

Chapter Five

Marco wasn't alone inside of his tent. Besides Donatello, who still sat inside the rabbit's trunk with that same blank expression—although this morning he had a black "CIRCUS MANAGEMENT" jacket draped over him—a very petite red-haired woman in a polka-dot lab coat was with him. A doctor's bag sat on the ground at her feet.

"Morning, Marco," I said as we joined them in the room. "How's Donatello doing?" I didn't ask about the jacket, figuring Marco must be worried about his brother growing cold from a lack of movement.

"The exact same as yesterday," Marco said. His eyes were bloodshot, his hair sticking up in tufts. "He won't drink or eat or sleep, so I called her." He pointed at the woman, who couldn't be more than four feet tall, if that. "This is Gigi," he said. "She used to work with us at another circus years ago before she retired to focus on her studies. She's a veterinarian now."

"I'm Electra." I shook Gigi's hand, which was as petite as the rest of her, yet her grip was strong. She smelled citrusy, with a hint of honey underlying it, reminding me of a magnolia blossom. She also smelled like a shapeshifter, but which breed I wasn't sure. A red feather stuck out of her hair. I figured it was either a clue to what she was post-shifting, or what she liked to eat. I thought about plucking the feather free, but decided it might be something she wanted there, so I left it.

"Electra is the sorceress I was telling you about," Marco said.

"I'm a seer, not a sorceress," I reminded him. "It's nice to meet you, Gigi." I pointed at her doctor's bag. "Did you figure out what's going on with Donatello?"

"Unfortunately, I couldn't find anything wrong with him." Her voice matched her size, sounding quite adorable. I liked this woman on sight. Whatever the color of her aura, it must be bright and cheery. "Besides being slightly dehydrated, of course."

"Marco," Bruno said, standing in the entryway leading back to the main room. "I'd like to search your office to see if I can find any clues as to who might be behind whatever is going on with your brother."

After a worried frown in his brother's direction, Marco left with Bruno following him, leaving Gigi and me alone.

"How long have you been a veterinarian?" I asked her, moving closer to Donatello. I waved my hand in front of his eyes. He didn't even blink. It was uncanny, really.

"A little over five years now," she answered, sitting down on the trunk I'd used yesterday as a stand for Ol' Blue. Her feet barely touched the ground.

"What's your specialty?" Some veterinarians preferred to work on larger animals. I'd had a great-uncle, though, who'd preferred to focus on exotic animals. When I asked him once why the exotics challenged him, he said they kept him from growing bored with the usual canines and felines.

"Shifters," Gigi answered, watching me with a narrowed look. "What's your breed, seer?"

"Werecoyote." I leaned closer to Donatello and sniffed his neck, and then bent down and sniffed his jacket at chest level. He smelled like a shifter ape, plain and simple.

"Mountain, plains, or desert region?"

"Desert. Southwest." I tried smelling his dominant arm and hand through his jacket, really focusing as I breathed in this time. Under his normal scent on the jacket, I noticed a faint odor of something slightly cedar-like with a sour edge, and yet woodsy, earthy even, especially near a muddy smear on the nylon fabric.

It reminded me of the swampy area at the southern fence line of our circus.

"You live here in Louisiana, right?" I assumed as much since Marco had pretty much pulled Gigi out of thin air this morning.

She nodded. "I find the regular humans down here in the bayou country far more accepting of our kind than those in many areas of the country."

I'd noticed the warmth and kindness as well in those natives who'd come to see our freakshow circus. Since she'd brought up that she was one of us, I asked, "What's your breed?"

"I come from the *Psittacidae* family."

"That sounds like a branch of the Sicilian mafia."

She laughed, a light tinkling sound that made me think of tiny bells. "Sorry, too much vet schooling. I'm a macaw hybrid."

I reached out and plucked that red feather from her hair. "Let me guess, a scarlet macaw?"

She nodded, taking the feather and stashing it in her lab coat pocket. "I seem to grow those even in my human form."

"I thought your kind was extinct." I'd read an article years ago about humans hunting them to capture and sell on the black market. Macaws made playful pets with their superb social interaction skills, especially the were-versions.

"Some varieties are close to it," Gigi said. "But we're not out of the game yet."

That was good to hear. "How well can you smell?"

Her nose was small like the rest of her, with a distinct curve at the end.

"Contrary to what most folks think, many birds have a well-developed sense of smell, myself included."

"Great." I described the scent I'd picked up on Donatello's sleeve to her. "Where do you think that came from?"

"Well, the sour, cedar-like smell is from the bald cypress tree, which dominates the swamps around here." She chewed on her lower lip. "The other scent might be Spanish moss, which grows on many trees, including the bald cypress." She looked at our patient, still squatting statue-like in his trunk. "You can smell all of that on him?"

I nodded. "Especially on the arm of his jacket."

She came over and sniffed. "Wow, you have an impressive nose on you."

"Once a coyote, always a coyote."

"Marco said you used your crystal ball last night to try to see into the past."

"I didn't get too far, but I did find where the bunnies who usually make a home in this trunk hopped off to."

"Did they smell like the swamp, too?"

"Not that I'd noticed, but I didn't bury my nose in their fur."

She walked closer and gently grabbed Donatello's lower lip, flipping it down. "If we don't get to the bottom of this by tomorrow, I'm going to need to pump him full of fluids intravenously."

"You've known Marco and Donatello for some time, huh?"

"Over a decade now. They sent me money to help pay for my schooling off and on when I was still in college."

"Do you know anyone from their past who might want to purposely harm Donatello? Someone he might have pissed off? Or to whom he owes money?"

"No. The monkey brothers are tight with their cash, but they are also big hearted and generous when someone is in need."

"Shoot." That didn't help me one bit.

"Listen, I could use some coffee." Gigi headed toward the main room. "You want to come with me? Or I could bring you one back if you'd rather stay here."

"Actually, I'd like to head over to their office car on the circus train and see if Bruno's found anything that could help." I frowned at Donatello. "You think we can just leave him there?"

"Sure. He's not going anywhere and most folks around here are still asleep. He'll be fine until Marco or I come back."

We stepped out into the sunlight and headed in separate directions after a smile and a wave. As I made my way through the tents to the train car that acted as the management office, I thought about Hank and Leon, trying to figure out how their incident might fit into the other oddities happening lately. In the end, I still couldn't make sense of it all and gave up. With any luck, Bruno had found something in the office.

Marco was sitting outside on the train car steps when I arrived. "You left Donatello with Gigi?" he asked.

"Actually, she went to get some coffee."

"You mean he's all alone?"

"Donatello is fine. Gigi said he could be alone for a bit."

Marco frowned. "If he was fine, he wouldn't still be in that damned trunk." He handed me a set of keys. "I'm going to go back and sit with him. Lock up when you and Bruno are finished."

"Will do." I patted him on the shoulder. "We'll figure this out," I said, trying to console him.

At least I hoped we would.

"Thank you, Electra." Marco pulled me into a clumsy hug and then raced off toward his tent.

Inside of the management office, I found Bruno perched behind the large mahogany desk that took up a third of the car. One of the previous managers had been a werebull and required a sizable desk for his massive, bulky form. According to Finn, when he'd quit and left for greener pastures higher up in management, he'd left the huge desk behind.

The rest of the place was filled with filing cabinets, two computers, and a printer. Whiteboards covered with details of scheduled town "jumps" and corresponding show dates covered the walls. I sat in one of the chairs opposite the desk. "Did you find anything that might clue us in on this mess?" I asked Bruno.

"No. Donatello has been busy with his lists and figures, though. Look at this." He held up a paper with several columns. "He wants Hank to keep track of how much time he spends scooping up shit. Can you believe that?"

"Maybe he was considering getting him an assistant," I said, trying to be positive. Donatello had offered the same to Eugene in one way or another, after all. I leaned back in the chair and crossed my legs.

Bruno lowered the paper along with his gaze, which got caught on my bare thighs at the hem of my mini-dress. "Are you wearing anything under that dress?"

I blinked at his question. "Yes, I'm wearing underwear. You saw me put this dress on, remember?"

His feral grin reminded me of the story of the big bad wolf. "How about you come over here and let me bend you over and check for myself?"

My libido sat up and took notice of his strong hands and sexy beard stubble, remembering how both felt on my bare skin. "Bruno Maska," I chided playfully. "We are supposed to be looking for clues right now."

His grin slipped. "Was that too obnoxious? Or vulgar? I didn't mean to make you feel harassed sexually. I suddenly had a risqué vision of taking you on this big desk. Not that I would do anything against your will, of course."

I groaned, wondering if whopping him upside the head with the stapler would stop this psychoanalysis madness.

"I'm doing it again, aren't I?" he asked, scowling.

"Yes, but I still love you." I pointed at the paper in his hand. "How about we focus on finding clues for now, and later I'll tie you to the bed, gag you with a silky veil, and ride you into the sunset." He loved it when I played cowgirl on him last week.

"Okay, but only if you feel comfortable doing that."

I tapped my index finger on the desk. "Shush and focus."

Half an hour later, I looked up from the filing cabinet where I'd been skimming through folders and noticed him staring down at a wrinkled shred of paper. "What's that?"

"I found it in the trash can. It's an address, I think. The name of the town is Crawfish Pie, if you can believe it?"

I walked over and looked at it, then moved to the bookshelf and pulled a road atlas from the shelf. The town was about twenty miles south-southeast, right smack dab in the middle of a swamp.

"You think this is Donatello's writing?" I asked, turning to Bruno, who was looking over my shoulder.

"I don't think. I know."

I smiled. "Good, then we have a clue. I wonder if Gigi will let us borrow her car." I assumed she must have arrived via a vehicle. If not, we'd have to improvise.

"You mean the vet in Marco's tent, right?"

"Yeah."

"Why do we need her car?"

"You and I are going to take a road trip to the swamp."

"What makes you think this address is something more than merely a local pitchman who supplies boudin balls and other local fare for the monkey brothers' food stand?"

"Because it's smack dab in the middle of the swamp, which is what I could smell on Donatello's jacket after you and Marco left their tent." I walked over to the office door, holding up the keys. "Come on, my majestic madman. Let's go wrestle some gators."

Chapter Six

It turned out Gigi the shapeshifting macaw did have a car, but it wasn't quite what I'd expected when Bruno and I had agreed that she could come with us to the swamp. The custom-made tiny clown car fit her small size perfectly. I, on the other hand, sat in the passenger seat with my knees touching my chin.

I glanced into the backseat at Bruno, who had climbed on board via the back hatch. The sight of him squeezed into the narrow confines of the tiny car reminded me of one of those cardboard tube packages of biscuit dough. If we popped a side window, he'd spill out onto the road.

Luckily for the two of us "big" shifters, we only had to endure the miniature torture chamber for twenty or so miles.

The town of Crawfish Pie was more of a collection of buildings to snag tumbleweeds—or it would have been if we were out west. Here in Louisiana, it appeared to be a nursery for Spanish moss on an island in the middle of the swamp.

"What's with the name?" Bruno asked as Gigi rolled along the road between a grouping of single-story homes tinged green with moss that bordered the bayou on their backsides.

"Once a year, this little town fills to the brim with people who come here to compete in the Best Crawfish Pie baking contest." She pointed at a long rectangular building on stilts. "The judges sit at tables inside the town's Royal Order of Alligators' Lodge and the pies are brought to them in groups of five." She smiled at me. "If you haven't tried crawfish pie, you should. They are mighty fine tasting."

I grimaced at the sound of a pie tin filled to the brim with crawfish, but I'd bet Eugene would be all over it like bees on honey. "Thanks, but I'll stick to beignets this trip and save the crawfish pie and alligator boudin balls for another go around."

"Damn," Bruno said from the back. "They sure are serious about their swamp boats around here. Look at the size of the propeller on that one to your right."

Holy gumbo! The blades were as long as Bruno was tall.

The place we were looking for was another mile up the road from Crawfish Pie's Alligator Lodge. It was more of a glorified shack than a house, with the plank siding long ago weathered gray. Mother Nature had added layers of varying greens over the years. Several large cypress trees bordered the old home. Spanish moss draped across their limbs to the roof, making it appear furry on top.

Gigi pulled into the limestone drive and killed the engine. "Now what?" she asked.

I frowned at a rocking chair up on the porch that was moving forward and backward without anyone sitting in it. "Now we find out if Donatello paid the owner of this place a visit recently, or if we've hit another dead end."

Gigi popped the back hatch and we spent a minute tugging Bruno out of the car. He stretched his back and neck once he was free, eyeing the car's roof racks. "Maybe you should tie me to the roof for the return drive."

"Funny and hunky." Gigi winked at me. "You're a lucky shifter."

When it came to having Bruno as my mate, sure—except when he was psychoanalyzing my moves in bed.

When it came to the bounty on my head, not so much. But that was a problem for another time.

The three of us approached the house at a slow pace, partly because the walkway was muddy with a healthy covering of leaf debris, but mostly because of the BEWARE OF GHOST DOG!

sign.

I wasn't sure if the owner was serious or had a good sense of humor. Personally, I didn't feel like finding out, but after a few sniffs of the air, I knew the scents around the place were what I'd picked up on Donatello's jacket earlier.

The porch boards groaned under our weight. There was no doorbell so I knocked on a rickety, wood-framed screen door. When nobody answered, Bruno knocked harder.

A metal creaking sound made me glance toward Gigi. She was peeking into a rusty mailbox nailed to the side of one of the porch posts.

"You know that's illegal, right?" Bruno asked, frowning.

"Yes, and normally I wouldn't peek in someone's mailbox, but look." She stepped aside and pointed at a piece of paper duct-taped to the outside of the box.

It read:

If you're a pick-up customer, check inside the box for your order.

"Is there anything inside?" I asked, joining Gigi at the mailbox.

"No. It's empty."

"Shoot."

"But look at this." She lifted the lid all of the way.

On the inside was a piece of masking tape with a phone number on it.

"Do you have a cell phone?" I asked her.

"It's in my purse in the car. I'll go get it." She headed back to the car.

"This place is sort of creepy," I said to Bruno.

He shot me a flirty grin. "It reminds me of one of those scream-queen movies where the teenagers sneak inside the spooky house on a dare, get all horny and start screwing around, and end up skewered like shish kebab while they're in the middle of knocking boots."

I rolled my eyes. "You need to pick up a novel more often."

He thumbed toward the house. "You want to go around back and act out one of the sex scenes from that book you've been reading?"

"Which one? One's erotica and the other is a modern-day western." Both were compliments of Eugene's library.

"We could compromise with a bit of both."

"Why, Bruno, are you trying to sex me up?" I whispered, fluttering my lashes at him.

He sobered. "Actually, I was trying to joke about screwing around, but I was probably being too crude. Maybe I should read some of Eugene's romance books to see how those guys seduce women. I've never been very good at the flowers and chocolate sort of wooing."

"Damn it, Bruno. You're overthinking this again."

He scowled. "Am I, though? You deserve the type of man who'd shower you with sonnets and expensive wine. Someone who'd take you out to fine restaurants."

I moved closer, speaking for his ears only. "Listen, I don't want any silly sonnets, and I certainly don't need wine. The last thing I need is to be drunk while professional killers are hunting me."

"Yes, but—"

I rolled my eyes at his *but*. "Bruno, I don't want to talk about this anymore." I stepped back, adding in a regular voice, "Let's go back to blood and guts."

"What about blood and guts?" Gigi asked, climbing the steps again, this time with her cell phone in hand. Her red hair gleamed in the dappled sunlight.

I noticed another red feather mixed amongst the tresses and smiled. "We were just discussing our favorite horror flicks," I lied, not wanting to share the current struggles Bruno and I were having when it came to mating. "Are you ready for the number?" At her nod, I lifted the metal mailbox lid and read the phone number to her.

She set the call on speakerphone so we could listen with her. After four rings, a husky female voice with a Cajun accent started talking:

> *Hey y'all. Dis is Patooty herself from Patooty's Booty Voodoo shop. If ya got dis message, den I'm on vacation at my sista's home in Haiti fa da whole month. Leave me a message an' I'll call ya when I git back ta good ol' Crawfish Pie.*

"Ah, hell," Bruno said when the message ended. "Of course she's on vacation. I bet she won't be back until our train jumps to the next town."

"Where are you heading next?" Gigi asked, tapping out something on her phone's screen.

"Armadillo, Texas," I told her, glancing back at the house. Bruno was probably right. Patooty hadn't left a number, so we'd come to the end of the line on this spur. "Well, on a high note, now we know what Donatello dilly-dallied with that landed him in that trunk. It was some sort of voodoo hoodoo."

"Hey, listen to this," Gigi said, reading from her phone's screen. "According to Patooty's website, she offers several spells and curses for purchase. Maybe Donatello bought one online and then came here to pick it up instead of having it delivered, since you guys are always rolling down the tracks."

"What kind of spells and curses?" Bruno asked, bending down to look over her head at the screen.

"Let's see, there are love spells, of course." She smiled at us. "Love Potion #9 would be at the top of my list."

"What else?" I pressed.

"Uhhh. Money spells. Luck spells—good and bad. Wish spells. Weight-loss spells. Protection spells. Transformation spells. And—wait!" She looked up. "Has Donatello been having any trouble with shapeshifting? Maybe he needs a boost to shift when the moon isn't full."

"Not that I know of," I said, turning to Bruno. "I would imagine that the monkey brothers would have come to me if so. They both confuse me for some kind of sorceress, thinking I have powers in addition to the gift of sight."

"Maybe they know something you don't," Gigi suggested.

I huffed. "I don't think so." Witchcraft and sorcery were not part of my DNA. "What about you, Bruno? Did the monkey brothers mention anything about trouble with shifting?"

"No. Nothing at all."

"Well, keep that spell in mind as a possibility," Gigi said. "Especially considering he's stuck in his wereape form at the moment. It could be why he came to Patooty."

"Good point." However, while that might explain why Donatello was playing wereape for so long, it didn't give a reason why he was taking up residence in that trunk. I crossed my arms. "What are some of the curses Patooty offers?"

Gigi scrolled her finger up her phone's screen. "There's a Revenge curse. It's listed near the top, so that must be a popular one. Here's a Banish Your Enemy curse." She grimaced. "Banish how, I wonder?" More scrolling on her part. "Here we go—the rest of the list. Patooty also offers an Ex-Lover's Rash curse, a Weight Gain curse, a Nose Growth for Lying curse, and a Constipation curse."

"Constipation and weight gain?" I wrinkled my nose at Bruno. "You'd better not piss me off, tough guy. Now I know where to go for payback curses."

His smile was wicked. "Yeah, but maybe I'll hit you with a love spell first so you'll find me adorable even when I'm being extra unruly."

"You two are cute," Gigi said. "What breed of shapeshifter are you?" she asked Bruno.

He hesitated, his eyes narrowing for a moment. "I'm a hybrid. My mother was a St. Bernard shifter and my father a full-bred werecoyote, like Electra here." He jammed his hands in his pockets. I knew from our pillow talk that the burr Bruno had about his father leaving before he was born still didn't sit well with him. Although he was less touchy about not being a purebred since we'd become a couple.

"Do coyotes mate for life like macaws do?" Gigi asked. "I can't remember that from my studies."

"I do," Bruno said. His eyes held mine, the love warming them spurring my heart to howl at the moon.

"Good answer," I said, patting him on the chest. "You're so well-trained already."

Bruno laughed and leaned against a porch post. "Tell me something, my sensationally seductive psychic. If Donatello was here and picked up a spell or a curse from Patooty's box, how will we find out what it is if he can't talk?"

I thought about that for a second.

"You know," Gigi said, stuffing her phone into her lab coat pocket, "I had an ex-boyfriend who swore his grandmother was a voodoo priestess and told me that she would often have her clients follow detailed written instructions."

I nodded. "Patooty's voice message said she'd be gone for the month, which is half over now. So maybe the spell or curse she left for Donatello was written down, which means we need to find where he put it."

"We have a plan," Gigi said, raising her fist in victory.

"Bruno, did you notice anything that looked like instructions for a spell or curse in the trash can where you found the address for this place?"

He shook his head. "The rest of the garbage was accounting-related paperwork and junk mail."

Prickly pears! "Let's head back to the circus. We still have time to search through Donatello's personal belongings before the gates open for tonight's show."

"Four hours and counting," Bruno said, pushing off the porch post. "I sure hope those bunnies in Finn's tent didn't eat Patooty's instructions when Donatello climbed into their trunk."

I crossed my fingers. "Me, too."

Chapter Seven

We made it back to the circus after one pit stop—a muscle in Bruno's lower back cramped and he had to stand up straight for a few minutes to stretch it out while I massaged away the pain.

"I'm never riding in that tiny tin can again," he said a few minutes later as we walked through the circus's employee entrance. "No offense, Gigi."

"None taken," she shot back with a grin. "Although I think the three of us crawling in and out of my car would make a great addition to the clowns' segment of the opening show."

"The little bird thinks she's funny," Bruno said to me. "I'm contemplating barking at her."

Gigi and I both laughed.

The sight of Eugene standing off to the side of the monkey brothers' food stand made us all take pause. It wasn't so much Eugene, who was still wearing his cutoff shorts with bulging pockets and T-shirt from earlier. It was his entourage, which now included a heron standing next to him with one leg raised and a barred owl perched on his shoulder. The skunk, two raccoons, and squirrel were grouped around him as he fed them French fries.

"More new friends, Eugene?" I asked, keeping a safe distance from his critters, especially the one with the long pointy beak.

Herons were deadly. I read an article once about how they took on alligators up to three feet long, stabbing them through the head with their beaks and then gulping them down whole. I might be outside of this bird's swallow-in-one-gulp range, but I had plenty of respect for that deadly sword attached to its face. I preferred my brain without holes in it.

"Yep. This guy flew into my tent after I returned from breakfast." He pointed a French fry at the owl on his shoulder. "He brought me a mouse for a snack, which I politely declined and set free."

"And the heron?" Bruno asked.

"Oh, she walked into my tent an hour ago, carrying the socks I was line-drying outside my tent. Then she picked up all of my dirty clothes from the floor and put them in my laundry basket. She's really handy, saving me from having to bend down. Watch this." Eugene dropped his paper napkin. The heron strolled over on its long spindly legs, skewered the napkin, and then dropped it off at the trash bin.

"Amazing," Gigi said. Only her eyes were on the werebear, not the heron.

Eugene nodded, smiling down at her. "I don't think we've met, little lady. I'd remember a face as beautiful as yours."

"Eugene, this is Gigi. She's a veterinarian who specializes in shapeshifters. Marco called her to come and take a look at Donatello."

"You're a vet?" His smile widened even further. "Well, call me pretty in pink. Before I was smitten, but now I'm in love."

Gigi's cheeks reddened, complimenting her hair. "Ah, you're just a really big flirt." She laced her fingers together in front of her. "Please, don't stop now."

"Your hair reminds me of the sun when it sits on the western horizon." He held up his bag of food. "Want to share some of my French fries?"

"I could eat one or two." She strolled toward where he sat on the bench. His animal entourage parted, leaving her a path to the spot next to him. "French fries are my second favorite finger food."

"Oh, yeah?" he said. "What's your first?"

"Crackers, of course. I like all kinds of them."

"I like crackers, too." His smile lit up his big face.

Ha! Eugene liked everything he could fit between his jaws. Now it appeared, he liked Gigi, too.

"We need to get moving," Bruno said in my ear.

"Gigi, we're heading over to the monkey brothers' tent," I told her. "You coming?"

She waved us off without taking her eyes off her seatmate. "You two go ahead. I'll join you later."

Bruno caught my wrist and pulled me along. I glanced back once to see Gigi leaning in as Eugene hand fed her a French fry.

"Oh, boy. How's that going to work?"

"They'll find a way," Bruno said. "Just like we did."

I smiled at him. The romance blossoming in the air between my friends filled me with the sweet scent of love, but then I remembered why we were heading for the monkey brothers' place. Reality smacked the hearts right out of my eyes.

Too bad I couldn't have picked up an enlightening spell from Patooty in Crawfish Pie to help me "see" a clue about whatever curse or spell that dang monkey purchased. How long did we have until Donatello's situation became dire? I couldn't imagine Marco continuing in the business without his brother, and while the two of them were pains in the ass when it came to bookkeeping, their hearts were kind and they came up with delicious recipes for their food stand. I'd hate to see them abandon the circus, leaving the rest of us to break in yet another new manager.

"Marco?" Bruno called when we reached their tent.

"Come in," Marco said, holding back the flap.

Inside, Finn stood in the middle of the main room while the monkey brothers' two tiny show bunnies hopped around his furry rabbit feet. The bunnies were making a high-pitched humming noise that almost hurt my ears. My excellent coyote hearing wasn't always a blessing.

"Did you make your deal?" I asked Finn, noticing his eyes were red rimmed, which I figured was from a few too many tokes last night.

Since the bunnies were back, I assumed Marco and he had come to some agreement about Finn's show remaining a once-a-night act. Although I was a little surprised that Finn didn't hold out longer to make the deal.

Marco's thick eyebrows raised. "What sort of deal?"

"I didn't bother," Finn answered. He glowered down at the bunnies. "After spending a night with these two assholes, I'm happy to give them back. No strings attached."

"What did they do to you?" Bruno asked, bending down to scratch one of the bunnies between the ears.

"It's what they didn't do, which was zip their lips and let me get some sleep." Finn rubbed his eyes, yawning before continuing. "All night long they crooned and chirped and caterwauled. At first I thought the high-pitched sound they were making was some sort of singing, which I initially found funny and cute. But after a couple of hours of it, that shit got old. So I put them in a box and turned off the lights, thinking about how the monkey brothers housed them in that dark trunk. But did they go to sleep? Oh, no. They made even more noise."

Marco scoffed. "These two are nocturnal."

"I noticed." Finn crossed his arms and thumped his back leg on the ground. "As soon as the lights were off, they started whistling and chattering, squeaking and grunting. They'd wait until I'd almost fall asleep, then they'd start with a new rhythm. I finally figured out that they were performing actual songs."

I looked at Marco. "I'd heard you and your brother had taught them to sing, but I figured it was just a note or two."

"Oh, they know all sorts of songs—from holiday tunes to 'Camptown Races.' " Finn yawned again. "These little buggers take that 'Goin' to run all night' line serious. They didn't shut up until the sun came up."

"Donatello has worked with them for months," Marco told

us. "He's trained them to perform multiple solos and duets. They're a rare breed of rabbit hailing from a region of Russia's far north that are known for their wide range of vocalization abilities."

"Well, wherever they're from, as far as I'm concerned you can ship them back home." He wiggled his whiskers at Marco. "You tell Donatello he needs to teach them the word 'quiet,' before someone else decides to silence them for good."

One of the bunnies looked up at him and made a high-pitched squeak. Finn bent down and held his fist in front of its tiny pink nose. "Keep it up, you little rat with tall ears."

"Come, now," Marco said, scooping it up. "They don't mean any harm. They just love to be heard."

"That's what they want you to think, apeman, but I know rabbits. Bugs Bunny wasn't rebellious by chance, you know." Finn backed away, his ears wilting at the tips. "If anyone needs me, I'm going to go take a nap in my tent before tonight's show so I don't fall asleep midway through my act."

After a nod in my direction, Finn hopped out of the tent without a backward glance. The two bunnies he'd been so keen to rescue from the monkey brothers' trunk yesterday watched him go, their noses twitching.

"Donatello will be happy to have these two troublemakers back." Marco scooped up the other bunny. "If he ever snaps out of his trance," he added with a wrinkled brow before carting the bunnies off to the side room.

I peeked through the curtains after him to check on his brother's status. Donatello was in the trunk still. Marco held up the bunnies in front of his brother's face. I watched for any reaction from Donatello, but there was none.

With a sigh, Marco placed the bunnies together in a large wooden bin, saying something under his breath to them before joining us back out front.

"Nothing's changed, I take it," I said.

He shook his head. "Donatello's stomach keeps growling,

though, so at least his body is working. Only his mind seems to have frozen."

"How do you feel about Electra and me taking a look through his personal effects in his kip?" Bruno asked, using the informal circus term for sleeping place.

Marco ushered us toward the curtain on the other side of the tent. "Have at it."

Bruno reached the curtain first. I stopped partway there and turned back. "Marco, did Donatello mention anything to you about going to see a woman named Patooty in Crawfish Pie?"

"No." He snorted. "Are those names real?"

"I'm afraid so." I left him standing with a perplexed expression on his face and joined Bruno in the room where Donatello slept when he wasn't spending the night in a trunk.

There wasn't anything fancy about the kip, unlike all of the veils and beads and candles in mine. Now I understood why Bruno struggled with the level of femininity I had draped throughout my sleeping quarters. Then again, my so-called girly stuff helped me to relax after a night of seeking out other folks' futures and pasts. It also eased my homesickness some, helping me to deal with the fact that the circus was where I belonged now, not the wide-open desert with its endless starry sky.

In this small, plain room, Donatello was simply looking for a place to crash each night. With his minimalistic budget mindset, a twin-sized cot, a wooden crate turned on its side for a nightstand, and an old army footlocker full of clothes probably suited him fine.

"There's not much here to search through, is there?" I asked Bruno, who was sifting through the clothes in the footlocker.

"No. It appears he's a miser both at work and leisure." He checked the pockets of a pair of blue jeans. "We should probably go through all of those trunks in the side room where they keep their magic stuff."

I sat on the cot and looked at the crate. Next to an old-fashioned monocle, a white candle weighted down a partially burned feather. The candle was small—too small to be of much use for reading. Then again, Donatello was probably too cheap to splurge on a larger one.

I pulled out the top hat that was tucked away inside of the crate, brushing the dust from the brim. The circus was always dusty, no matter if we were in humid areas or on the dry prairie. With all of the people and animals coming and going, the air was continually stirred.

I smiled at the hat. Donatello wore it for their opening act. From what Lolli told me, it was a gift from the brothers' mother for their first show long ago. Turning the hat over, I admired the red silk lining, impressed at how clean and colorful it was after so many years. The tag on the inner lining caught my eye. Three sides of it were sewn on with black thread rather than the red thread used on the fourth side. The black thread looked rather crooked, too, with one of the corners coming loose. I reached inside the hat and tugged on the corner of the tag. It came loose from the strip of Velcro holding it in place.

Velcro? On a hat this fancy?

I pulled harder. Underneath it, was a hidden pocket. Ahhh, was this part of their magic act? What would Donatello be able to hide in such a small pocket, though?

"Bruno," I said, slipping two fingers inside of the pocket.

He looked up from the footlocker as I extracted a small piece of folded paper. "What's that?"

My fingers trembled slightly as I unfolded it. I scanned the words, my pulse skipping. "I think it's the spell instructions."

He joined me as I read the handwritten scrawls:

> First, burn the white inscribed candle while reciting:
> *To accomplish for me this feat, I will dutifully repeat.*

> Second, burn the egret feather while chanting three times: *What I desire, I will acquire.*

> Third, burn this piece of paper and sprinkle the

ashes into a well while chanting: *This spell will stick until I …*

The rest of the paper was burned so I couldn't finish it.

"Damn it," I whispered. "This is the spell he got from Patooty." I sniffed the paper.

"What do you smell?"

"Burned paper. It's overpowering everything else." I pointed at the candle and partially burned feather on the crate next to the cot. "He started the spell, but didn't finish it."

"What's that mean? That it didn't take? Or is that the trouble?"

"I don't know in this case, but when I was a kid, a witch paid a visit to my grandmother. She was an old friend and I remember asking her if she could do a spell that would make me taller. My grandmother interrupted and warned me to be careful with spells. She said that if they were performed incorrectly, they could backfire and the result might be undesirable."

"No shit." He sat on the cot. "You believe that these spells of Patooty's truly work?"

"Bruno, I'm a fortune teller. Do you really think I don't believe?"

"Right. Stupid question." He sighed. "So, what now? We know Donatello picked up a spell from Patooty and that he started to go through with it. How does that explain him sitting in that trunk in the other room like some sort of voodoo zombie?"

"I don't know. Maybe—"

A commotion of voices in the other room interrupted me. I heard my name in the mix, followed by a streak of curses.

"Now what?" I whispered.

Bruno stood. "Only one way to find out." He left me standing alone next to Donatello's cot.

I tucked the spell back in the top hat, returned it to the crate, and raced after him.

Chapter Eight

I peeked out through the curtain to find out who had come looking for me before allowing myself to be spotted.

Bruno was playing bouncer on my behalf, blocking a portion of my view with his broad shoulders. Marco was partially hidden behind Bruno, but I spotted the source of the commotion.

Hank and Leon had paid a visit. The former was standing with his hands next to his narrow hips while Leon circled him, brushing his blond stubbly cheek against Hank's upper arm periodically. Both were in their human forms, but their body movements and gestures parodied ape and feline to the extreme.

"I know she's here somewhere," Leon said, pushing his thick mane of blond hair back and lifting his nose to sniff the air. "I can smell her, dammit."

"Listen, Marco," Hank cut in, his voice deep and growly. His black uni-brow made a straight line across his bulging forehead. "We just need to talk to her for a few minutes. That's all. Leon is really screwed up, and I can't take much more of him rubbing all over me like this." He grabbed Leon by the scruff of his shirt collar and hauled him away, pointing at the nearby chair. "Sit over there, cat."

"Leon isn't the only one!" Marco snapped. "Donatello hasn't had food or water in over twenty-four hours."

Crap. This was getting serious. I dodged Bruno, stepping into the fray.

"You look okay to me," I said, looking down at Leon, who

was smoothing his hair where Hank had messed it up.

Leon took both of my hands in his, his face pinched as he lowered to his knees on the floor. "Oh, Electra," he wailed. "I need your help. I can't stop thinking about Hank."

I raised my eyebrows. "You mean romantically?"

He shook his head, his blond mane flowing, tempting me to reach out and pet him. "I feel like I need to be near him all of the time and I can't stop touching him. Even worse, I have a strong urge to crawl up on his lap and purr. What's wrong with me? Please tell me this is just some horrible ailment that will pass soon."

"Hey now," Hank said, his wedge-shaped jaw jutting. "There's no need to be hurtful."

"Please don't be mad at me, Hank." Leon crawled over to the gorilla shifter again, purring while rubbing against his bowed legs.

Hank cursed at the tent ceiling. "See what I mean," he said to Marco, trying to hold Leon at bay. "Electra, you need to look into your ball and figure out what's going on with Leon. He's out of control."

I shot Bruno a worried glance before turning my attention back on the two visitors. "You guys don't happen to know a woman named Patooty from Crawfish Pie, do you?"

"No, should I meet her?" Leon asked, struggling to break free of Hank's grip. "Will she help me get over the unstoppable need to mark Hank with my scent?"

"Maybe. Unfortunately, she's on vacation."

"Of course she is." Hank let go of Leon and pointed at the chair again, this time with more emphasis until Leon obeyed. Hank turned back to me. "After putting up with Leon's claws digging into my back and his fur up my nose for the last twelve hours, I've changed my mind."

"About what?" Marco asked.

"My wish for a kitten. I'll settle for my rhinoceros and elephants. They may not be as cute and cuddly as a kitty, but at least they don't try to crawl onto my lap every time I sit down."

In spite of the seriousness of the situation, the idea of Leon curled up on Hank's lap made me grin.

"It's not funny, Electra," Hank said, apparently reading my mind.

"Sorry. You're right, none of this is." I motioned toward the tent flap. "If you two will follow me back to my tent, I'll …"

Wait a second!

I turned back to Hank. "What did you just say?"

"This shit with Leon isn't funny."

"Before that."

He thought for a moment. "That Leon's desire to sit in my lap all the live-long day is a pain in the ass."

"Not that part, the part about wishing."

"My wish for a kitten?" he asked.

"Yes! That part. When?"

"When what?"

"When did you wish for a kitten?"

He shrugged. "I don't know. I do it all of the time. Kittens are so darn cute with their adorable little meows and big bright eyes. I've been keeping an eye on the local papers as we travel, but it's the wrong time of year."

I waved off all of that other fluff he'd said. "Did you *recently* wish for a kitten?"

He scratched his hairy cheek. "Uh, yeah. Yesterday, as a matter of fact. I was shoveling out the elephants' pen and thinking how much easier it would be to have a kitten for a pet with a litter box."

I snapped my fingers. "That's it," I said to Bruno.

"What's it?" Marco asked.

"It's Patooty's Wish spell."

"Are you sure?" Bruno asked, his dark gaze edged with skepticism. "This was Hank making the wish, not Donatello."

"I know, but think about it. Hank wished for a kitten. The wish was granted, sort of—instead of a kitten, a werelion showed up on his doorstep."

"More like in my bed," Hank grumbled.

That reminded me of another wish I'd heard with my own ears. "Yesterday, before showtime, Eugene was in my tent and wished for an assistant because he's having trouble lighting the matches for his flaming torch performance."

Bruno nodded. "And now he's covered with helpers."

"Exactly. They not only light his flaming torch, but they're bringing him food, cleaning his house, helping him dress, and picking up stuff for him."

"Yes, but how—" Bruno started.

"And you!" I interrupted him, my mind really latching onto this idea now.

He grimaced, glancing toward the other three watching us. "What about me?" he asked in a lowered voice.

"You wished to stop analyzing other things and focus on ..." He'd mentioned me and my body, but I could see by his warning squint that I needed to step carefully in front of the others with this personal subject. "And focus on me," I finished.

He scoffed. "That wish certainly blew up in my face. Patooty's spell doesn't work for shit."

"That's not true," I said. "The wishes were granted, only they came out sort of crooked."

"Crooked." Marco repeated with a glower. "Do you think this Patooty's Wish spell is similar to the wishes in that old story, 'The Monkey's Paw'? The wishes made in it are granted, but at a high personal price."

"Weren't there three wishes granted in that tale?" Hank asked.

"Just like we've had three granted," Leon added.

"No, four." Bruno pointed toward the side room. "Donatello is still mute in that trunk. For all we know, other folks will be coming to Electra for help soon because of more wishes gone south."

I paced, thinking this through. "Okay, so we know that in addition to Hank wishing for a kitten, Eugene wishing for an assistant, and Bruno wishing he could stop analyzing things,

Donatello wished for something, but he didn't finish the wish spell per the instructions and now he's squatting in a trunk in a catatonic state."

"What do you think his wish was for?" Leon asked.

Hank huffed. "Knowing that skinflint, it was probably to have everyone detail their daily activities in fifteen-minute intervals on a time schedule to see where we could save time that could be used to do other work."

"Hey!" Marco stuck his chest out toward Hank, pounding it twice. "We're talking about my brother here."

"Careful, li'l apeman," Hank said, puffing his own chest out in response. "Remember who stands taller on the hominid family tree."

"Cool it, you two," Bruno warned, stepping between the two wereapes. "Or I'll bite you both on the ass."

"*Talking* is certainly what Donatello does best," Leon said, breaking the tension in the room. "He stopped by the day before yesterday and wouldn't shut up about how I've been going through too much gas during my chainsaw juggling act."

"Gas?" I asked, shaking my head yet again at Donatello's penny-pinching.

"Can you believe he wants me to buy an electric chainsaw?" Leon wrinkled his upper lip. "He doesn't understand that the sound of a gas chainsaw is part of the wow factor."

Bruno smirked. "I think you're forgetting the fact that the King of the Jungle is juggling deadly tools with his bare paws."

Wouldn't shut up, *Leon's voice repeated in my thoughts. I looked toward the side room where Donatello and the rabbits were currently taking up residence, hearing Finn's voice* … They won't shut up.

"The Russian bunnies," I said to Marco, an idea taking form.

Marco frowned. "What about our show bunnies?"

"Does Donatello practice with them before your show?"

"Yes, sometimes." Marco scratched his chin. "Wait, now that I think about it, Donatello had been working on a new tune for the bunnies to sing lately. Just the other night he complained to me about how they kept singing their own songs and wouldn't listen to him."

"Ah ha!" I held up my index finger. "Maybe Donatello made a wish about the bunnies."

"And that's why he's in the bunny trunk?" Bruno asked.

I could tell by his face that he was having trouble swallowing this new idea. "Hear me out. Maybe the same thing happened to him as with the rest of you—something backfired, and now he's stuck in their trunk and can't tell us why."

"That sounds a bit farfetched," Leon said, grooming his hair again.

"That's rich coming from a grown man who keeps trying to sit on my lap," Hank shot back.

"If you're right," Bruno cut in, "then we have a bigger problem. Somehow that screwed-up Wish spell is spreading throughout the circus and we need to figure out how to stop it."

"Yeah." I grimaced. "That's where we hit a snag."

"Can't you fix it, Electra?" Hank asked. "I thought you were some kind of great sorceress."

I rolled my eyes. "I'm a seer, not a sorceress."

"Close enough," Leon said.

Not really. Not at all. "Listen, I'm not a voodoo priestess or a witch or a sorceress, so get that idea out of your thick heads." I shot a worried frown at Bruno. "The bottom of the spell instructions were singed, but Donatello didn't follow through and burn the whole paper, nor dump the ashes down a well. Unfortunately, unless we can figure out what the last part of the spell said and finish the job for him, I don't know how we're going to stop it."

"Oh, Donatello." Marco covered his mouth. "What have you done?"

"Until I can figure this puzzle out," I told them all, "nobody should make any wishes."

"But what do we do about my brother?" Marco said, twisting his hands together. "He needs nourishment and liquids."

"I don't know, Marco." I chewed on my lower lip. "We can start with finding Gigi. She'll know how to keep him hydrated for now."

Bruno started for the exit. "I'll bring her back here. Hank, stay with Electra."

"What about me?" Leon asked.

"Do some investigative work for me," Bruno said, pausing at the tent flap. "Ask around and see if anyone else's wishes are coming true—sort of. We need to keep track of how far this spell has spread."

Leon left shortly after Bruno, leaving Hank, Marco, and me to wait for their return. Marco went to check on his brother. Hank followed, asking if he could play with the bunnies while we waited, to which Marco agreed. The tension between the two wereapes had apparently eased as quickly as it coiled.

I stayed where I was and paced the four corners of the tent, going through the screwy situation we were in again and again, trying to come up with a solution.

Marco was right to be worried about his brother. Time was running out for Donatello, and with Patooty off vacationing in Haiti, that left me as the go-to guru for voodoo spells. The problem was, I didn't know much about voodoo. I'd grown up with a seer out west, far away from the world of the Haiti-based religion. Maybe I could log onto the internet in the monkey brothers' office and see if there was some sort of local voodoo priest or priestess who could help us out of this bind.

Then again, maybe the interference of another voodoo envoy would make this screwy Wish spell even worse somehow.

I pounded the heel of my palm against my forehead. "Think, Nora," I said, dropping into one of the chairs. "How do I fix this?"

If I didn't come up with something soon, Donatello could end up in the hospital, drawing the attention of local authorities, which was the monkey brothers' worst nightmare.

Not to mention that Eugene would be overrun with the local

wildlife soon. With his luck, one of those critters would probably give him rabies by accident.

And then there was Leon. The poor werelion would have to put his nightly act on hold until he could focus on juggling chainsaws instead of Hank or else risk cutting off his paw. Or worse.

I blew out a breath, letting my hands dangle between my knees. Of course I couldn't forget about Bruno, who was going to drive me stark raving mad with his over-thinking about our relationship. How long until his psychoanalysis of everything in our love life started interfering with his day job? The head of security needed a clear head to keep this circus in line. AC had a reputation for her lack of tolerance when it came to blunders from her immediate subordinates.

"Great balls of fire," I said, scowling at the curtain leading to Donatello's kip. "This is a fine mess you landed us in, monkey."

What had the ape shifter been thinking? Didn't he know better than to fiddle around with voodoo? Hadn't anyone ever told him to be careful what he wished for?

Chapter Nine

By the time Bruno returned with Gigi, I had changed my mind about an earlier idea.

"How about we contact another voodoo priest and see if the Wish spell could be reversed somehow?"

Gigi got on board with my idea right out of the gate, pulling out her cell phone. "That sounds like a plan. Let me see if I can find someone online with an emergency voodoo phone number."

Bruno, on the other hand, had a face lined with doubt. "Do you really thi—"

Before he could finish, I added, "If annulling the spell isn't possible, then maybe they can supply another spell that overpowers the first."

The doubt lines deepened. "Don't you think we've screwed around with this voodoo shit enough for now? What if we make things even worse with another spell?"

There was that chance. "If you have a better idea, Bruno the Wise, I'd love to hear it."

He stared at me for several seconds, his expression tightening into a stony scowl. "We're playing with people's lives here, Electra, especially Donatello's. You of all people should know that dabbling with voodoo can lead to death—or something even worse, from what I've read." He ended with a grimace.

"Since when did you start reading?" I teased with a playful smile, trying to reduce the friction building between us. "When I agreed to be your fated mate, I was under the impression that you were heavy on the brawn and light on the brains."

His sudden grin broke the surface tension on his face. "Apparently, your crystal ball failed you during that particular scry, oh fortune teller." His gaze traveled south to my cleavage. "Or some voodoo priestess sold you a bad-luck bag of *gris-gris*."

Scry *and* gris-gris? That was jargon from my line of work, not his. "Why, Bruno dear. You've been studying."

He winked. "Yes, I have. Up close and personal, especially late at night in the candlelight with the help of a very thorough tutor."

"Here's one!" Gigi said, interrupting our flirting match. She held up her cell phone. "Queen Zabette. Voodoo has been in her blood for five generations."

Bruno's scowl returned. "Shouldn't we have a more thorough vetting process than a quick internet search?"

"She's averaging 4.6 stars out of five with over 700 reviews," Gigi added. "That's an impressive score."

"Does she have a phone number?" I asked.

Bruno walked away, shaking his head.

"Yep. It's toll free. You want me to call it now?"

I glanced at Bruno, who stood with his back to us. "Yes."

Gigi tapped the screen and held the phone out for me to take.

"For the record," Bruno said, turning to face us, "I think this is a mistake."

"Duly noted," I said and took the phone.

"Queen Zabette's Voodoo hotline," a wheezy voice answered, the woman on the other end sounding five generations old herself.

I took a deep breath and spilled our story.

Ten minutes later, I hung up the phone.

"Well?" Gigi bounced. "Did she give you a new spell?"

"No." I handed her back the phone.

"Did she know the last line of our Wish spell?" Bruno asked.

I shook my head, frowning toward the room where Donatello

sat on his haunches waiting for us to rescue him.

"What did she say?" Bruno pressed, returning to my side.

"Basically, we're screwed."

"Oh, no." Gigi covered her mouth.

"She said that the only way to fix this was to finish the Wish spell. When I asked about her giving me a new line to replace the part that's burned, she said that she couldn't do that. Only the original spellmaker can supply that line. Otherwise, the spell would be a mutant of the first and could result in even more chaos, possibly even death."

"Son of a bitch." Bruno dropped into one of the armchairs, muttering under his breath, "Damned meddling monkey."

"So now what?" Gigi asked, picking up her doctor's bag. "I mean, I can give Donatello fluids intravenously, but that's only a bandage. If we can't snap him out of this soon, I'm going to have to take him to a hospital." Her brow pinched. "You know how that will end for a shifter in a nearly vegetative state, right? At best, he'll be put in a facility and strapped to a bed for the rest of his life as his muscles atrophy and he slowly dies. At worst, he'll end up in an experimentation lab. The exact kind of place his mother worked so hard to free him and Marco from."

"Shit," I said. The weight of what had seemed so amusing at first sat heavy on my chest. Time was running out.

Bruno stood. "I need to go help out at the front gates. We open in ten minutes."

I sighed. I'd forgotten that we all had a circus to run. "Who's going to start the show?"

"I am," Marco said from the threshold to the other room. He wore his magician's cape and hat. "Donatello would agree that no matter the situation, the show must go on."

I walked over and gave him a hug. "I'll figure something out."

He patted my back as he held me. "You've done your best, Electra. Remember, this was not your doing." He pushed me back, staring down at me with watery eyes. "If Donatello's fate is to end in a lab, so it shall be. You've tried to help, and for that he and I are forever grateful."

I blinked the tears from my eyes and stepped back. "I'm not giving up yet."

Bruno took my arm. "Come on, sweetheart. It's time to go to work." He led me outside under the warm sunshine, but I shivered anyway.

We walked back to my tent in silence as the circus hustled and bustled around us, our coworkers preparing to deliver another night of mystery and awe.

My mind churned, trying to come up with a solution. "There has to be something I can do to help."

Bruno pulled me to a stop outside of my tent flap. "I need to go to work, Nora, but I feel like I need to stay with you and talk about all of this."

I patted his chest. "While I appreciate the gesture, talking about your feelings is not your cup of tea."

"Tell me about it, yet here I stand at your service." He scoffed. "I think this stupid Wish spell pumped me full of estrogen."

"That's a sexist thing to say." I tried to lighten things a little.

His mouth drooped at the corners. "You're right. Now I feel bad about that."

I laughed, which felt good for the few seconds it lasted. I kissed him. "Go to work, big dog. We can 'talk' later."

Without a backward glance, I slipped inside my tent and headed for my private quarters. It was time to change into Madam Electra's peasant blouse and long velvet skirt and get busy telling fortunes. As Marco had said, we had a show to put on for paying guests. No matter how dire things were behind the scenes, one thing all of us shifter freaks were good at was pretending.

It was nearing midnight by the time I made it to the end of my line of customers. My tip jar overflowed with gratuities. For whatever reason, tonight had been themed with happy endings for those whose futures I sought. Too bad the same couldn't be said for Donatello.

I started to put away Ol' Blue and then stopped, putting it back on its stand and lowering into my chair again. I had to try one more time for the monkey brothers. Clearing my thoughts, I hovered my fingers over the blue sphere, waiting until the moment felt right to make contact. I opened my mind, ready to receive, but before I laid my hands on the ball, I heard Queen Zabette's wheezy voice speak in my head loud and clear:

You must finish the Wish spell …

I lowered my hands to the table.

That was it!

Of course, now it seemed so simple.

I stood and stuffed Ol' Blue in its lockbox, tucking it under the parlor table until tomorrow night.

Holding up my long skirt, I rushed out of my tent and ran toward the monkey brothers' tent.

I passed Eugene and his entourage on the way, doing a double take at the sight of a four-foot-long alligator zigzagging along behind the rest of the werebear's crew of critters.

"Where's the fire?" Eugene called after me.

"I think I know how to save Donatello," I yelled over my shoulder.

"Can I help?"

"Yes. Find Bruno." I paused long enough to add, "Tell him to meet me at the monkey brothers' place."

Upon reaching their tent, I jogged inside without waiting for an invitation. Marco was pacing between the two armchairs while Gigi prepped a bag of clear fluid that I figured was for Donatello. They both looked at me in surprise.

"I know … what … to do," I told them between gulps of air.

"To help Donatello?" Marco asked, his eyes wide, hopeful.

I nodded and held up a finger as I waited for my lungs to

catch up with my feet. I really needed to stop sitting on my butt so much in my parlor chair and do some exercise. Bruno went for a run every other morning. Maybe I could join him. I thought about how nice it was to crawl back between the sheets after I did my daily sunrise greeting. Then again, maybe I'd ease into exercising with a walk around the big top tent periodically.

Bruno showed up just as I was ready to explain my idea. The brute wasn't even winded, dang it. "Eugene said you figured out how to end this spell."

"It's obvious, really," I told him and the others. "I need to make a wish."

"No." Bruno didn't even take a moment to think about it.

"I know what to wish," I assured him.

"It's a bad idea."

"At least hear me out."

"I don't like it."

I growled, crossing my arms. "Bruno, stop being so damned stubborn and listen."

He huffed, but nodded once, giving me the go-ahead.

"Queen Zabette told me that to fix this mess, we needed to finish the Wish spell. I understood her to mean that we needed that last line to finish it, but we don't."

"We don't?" Marco asked.

I shook my head. "All I have to do is make a wish that will nullify all of the previous wishes."

My idea was met with silence for several ticks.

Marco was the first to speak. "You really think something that simple will bring Donatello back to us?"

"Maybe," I said with what I hoped was a positive smile.

"Maybe?" Bruno grimaced at Gigi. "*Maybe*, she says." He growled and dropped into one of the armchairs.

"What if it doesn't work?" Gigi asked, setting the fluid bag on the arm of her chair.

"Well, then we aren't any worse for wear, are we?"

"*You* could be," Marco said.

"Especially if your wish goes sideways like everyone else's," Bruno added.

"If it does," I returned, still smiling, "then we'll figure out how to get hold of Patooty."

"That could mean taking a side trip to Haiti," Gigi said.

"So be it."

"Electra," Marco said, "I don't want you to risk yourself for Donatello. He wouldn't want that either."

"We're a family here," I told him. "This is the sort of thing you do for those you care about and want to help."

He frowned, but then nodded. "Okay. I trust you with Donatello's life."

Whoa, that was a heavy weight. I adjusted my shoulders to carry the burden.

"I'll help however I can," Gigi volunteered with a warm smile.

I looked to Bruno. "And you?"

He blew out a breath, his dark gaze steady on mine. "You really believe this could work?"

"I do."

"Then I have your back, babe."

After I blew him a kiss, I headed for the other room where Donatello stood in the trunk.

Marco followed, hovering near his brother. Gigi joined us next to the trunk, her doctor's bag in hand, ready to help if the wereape finally snapped out of his catatonic state. Bruno stood in the doorway with his arms crossed, his legs in a wide stance.

"Everyone cross your fingers," I said, straightening my shoulders.

"You're not exactly inspiring confidence," Bruno teased.

"Have faith in the seer, Sir Skeptic." I took a deep breath, blew it out, and closed my eyes.

After several beats of silence, I was ready. Keep it simple, I thought, and said, "I *wish* to negate all effects from Patooty's incomplete Wish spell."

I waited with my eyes still closed for a sign that something had changed.

"I wish to abolish the Wish spell's existence," Gigi added, surprising me into opening my eyes. She shrugged at my raised brows. "I thought maybe we could use some added insurance."

"Was that wise?" Marco asked, frowning down at Gigi. "We don't know if Electra's wish worked yet."

"Electra's wish for what?" came a rusty voice from the box.

I gasped.

"Donatello?" Marco stepped toward his brother, who was kneeling in front of the box in his naked human form except for the black circus jacket he'd still been wearing. "Are you okay?" He pulled a black magician's cape from one of the magic trunks and draped it over his brother's trembling shoulders.

The other monkey brother rubbed his throat. "I'm dying of thirst."

"Yes, you were," Gigi said, rushing over with her bag.

"Gigi," Donatello said, blinking at her. "I dreamed about you." He looked beyond her, his gaze landing on me. "And you, too, Electra." His thick eyebrows drew together when they landed on Bruno. "And that somebody kept poking me in the cheek."

Bruno raised his hands. "I'm innocent." At my narrowed look, he added, "Well, I was, until Electra wrangled me into submission." He grinned at me, a wicked glint in his eyes.

In that glint, I saw a glimpse of good old Bruno, the alpha version, who hated to talk about his emotions.

While Marco and Gigi tended to Donatello, I walked over to Bruno, lowering my voice for his ears only. "How are you feeling?"

He cocked his head to the side, taking a moment to answer. "I'm not sure."

"Do you want to go somewhere alone with me and talk about our relationship?"

He cringed. "Hell, no." His gaze dropped to my lips. "But I wouldn't mind going somewhere alone with you and practicing a little 'seeing' of my own." He leaned closer. "We can start with you getting naked while I do some intense 'readings' of your body with my palms and fingers." His hands slid down over my hips, pulling me closer. "Then, if you open up to me about *your* deep feelings, I'll show you what I foresee in your immediate future."

I chuckled. "It's good to have you back and trying to sex me up."

"Bruno," Gigi interrupted. "We need your help moving Donatello to his bed so I can examine him further and give him a dose of fluids. He's pretty dehydrated."

"What happened to me?" Donatello asked.

"That's a good question," Bruno said, crossing the room to help Marco lift his brother. "One that Electra and I will be stopping by in the morning to talk to you about after you've had some rest."

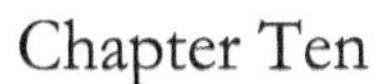

Chapter Ten

Bruno and I waited in the monkey brothers' tent for another fifteen minutes while Gigi gave Donatello a quick checkup. After Marco told us all was as well as could be after the ordeal, we strolled through the dark, quiet circus toward our tent.

"You think we should stop by Eugene's?"

"Why?"

"To make sure his entourage hasn't turned on him. He could be cornered in his tent right now."

"Nora." Bruno laced his fingers through mine. "I'll remind you that Eugene shapeshifts into a grizzly bear. I think he can handle a few small forest creatures, even if they get a little aggressive with him."

"But he had an alligator following him around earlier."

Bruno chuckled. "I know. I saw the toothy bastard when Eugene came to get me. You should be more worried about his entourage turning on each other. Owls hunt skunks and herons kill gators."

I crossed my fingers there wasn't a bloodbath going on in Eugene's tent.

"I'm more concerned about Hank and Leon," Bruno added. "When I talked to the two of them a few hours ago, Hank was threatening to personally declaw Leon with a pair of pliers if the werelion didn't stop flexing his claws while sitting on Hank's lap."

I giggled. "Those two make quite a pair."

He draped his arm over my shoulders. "Leon found a few more, by the way."

"A few more what?"

"Shifters who'd made wishes. Nothing had happened as major as what Donatello experienced, thankfully. I'll make the rounds in the morning and make sure everything has settled back to normal for those affected."

I leaned my head against his shoulder. "It was too easy."

"You mean getting me into bed the first time or dispelling the wish?"

"Both."

"Yeah, but with me you cheated."

"What?" I smiled up at him. "How?"

"You got me drunk and then took advantage of me."

"Took advantage, my ass." I poked him in the side, making him grunt and laugh. "You were egging me on that night, pushing my buttons, practically daring me to kiss you."

"True. It took you long enough to shut me up with those sexy lips of yours."

We reached my tent. He held the flap for me, following me through the waiting area and then the curtain leading to my parlor. There he caught my arm and pulled me toward him. "How about I push some more of your buttons, Madam Mayhem."

"Hmmm," I pretended to think about it.

"There's that *hmmm* again."

"Is there going to be any kissing first?"

"There'd better be," he said, cupping my face with his hands.

"Are you going to want to analyze my moves?"

"No."

"What about orgasms?"

He raised his brows. "What about them?"

I grinned. "Will we have to stop to talk afterward about how they made us feel?"

"Smartass," he whispered and lowered his mouth to mine.

There was no talking then, only groans and moans as he took his time teasing and tempting while his hands traveled over hill and dale. He undressed me slowly, loosening the strings on my peasant blouse as he tasted my neck. Then he picked me up and took me to bed. There, our clothes came off piece by piece, starting with mine and ending with his.

He stayed true to his word, taking me to the moon and back with his hands and fingers, keeping me silent with his kisses the whole time. Then, while my heart was still pounding, he slid into me, pushing deep.

He caught my gasp with his mouth. He growled in his throat when I wrapped my legs around his hips and clawed at his back.

I pulled away from his kisses long enough to ask, "How do you want it?"

"I just want it, period." He slid out and in again, his face soft with desire. "Now zip it, woman. We've talked enough."

I laughed and scraped my nails down his arms, my hips moving with his. "Is that all you got?"

It wasn't. The way his mouth worked mine as his body moved within me was intoxicating. This time, our mating was more sensual, taking me to a higher level physically than I'd experienced before with him. I bowed under him when my pleasure peaked, my whole body pulsing with delight.

He joined me on the other side of pleasure shortly after I'd come back to earth, his arms and legs trembling still when he collapsed on top of me. We lay in silence afterward, our breathing loud in the darkness.

He rolled onto his back, pulling me along and settling me on top of him. "Damn, Nora. If I were to keel over right now, I'd die an incredibly happy, satisfied man."

I rested my cheek on his chest, listening to his heart as it slowed to an even tempo. "Bruno?"

"Yeah?"

"I have an idea."

"If it involves the two of us naked on your parlor table, you need to give me a little time to catch my breath."

I smiled, stroking the skin on his arm. "How about when we set up the tent after the next jump, we decorate our private quarters with your stuff."

"I don't have any stuff."

"You must have a few personal items somewhere, like a picture of your family, or a trophy or some mementos from your previous life before the circus."

"Nora."

"What?"

"I like being surrounded by your things."

"But you said they're girly."

"They remind me of you, soft and sexy."

I scooted up his chest, bracing on my arms so I could look down into his eyes. "But Bruno …"

He placed his finger over my lips. "Of course, if you want to drape your lacy panties and bras all over the room, I'm good with that, too."

I snorted. "That's the Bruno I know and love."

His gaze held mine, the tenderness I could see in his eyes making my body want to sing and dance to his tune all over again. "The only thing I want to change in this room," he said, "is to add some things that symbolize the two of us."

"Like what? Pictures?"

He shrugged. "Treasures that we find together, for example."

"That's very romantic, Bruno." I kissed him. I couldn't resist.

When I came up for air, he said, "Nora Mai, why are your hips moving like that?"

"I've had a vision."

"Of what?"

"Let me show you."

He folded his arms behind his head and watched through half-closed eyelids as I worked my magic on his body. After he'd seen enough, he gave me a performance of his own that filled me with wonder yet again at the new heights of satisfaction I reached from his touch.

Sleep came quickly in the ensuing silence. I woke right before dawn as usual, my internal alarm having been set long, long ago.

When I returned from greeting the sun, Bruno was up and pulling on his jeans.

"Where are you off to?"

"I want to check on the others who'd been screwed up by Patooty's Wish spell." He glanced at the clock on my nightstand. "How about you meet me at the monkey brothers' food joint in an hour for coffee and beignets?"

"Twist my arm." That would give me time to take a long shower and organize my parlor room.

"See you in a bit, Madam Knock-My-Socks-Off." He gave me a kiss good-bye and strode out before I could think of a cheeky reply.

I showered, dressed, and prepped for another night of fortune-telling. Bruno was waiting for me with a bag of beignets and hot coffee mixed with chicory when I joined him at the monkey brothers' stand.

"I like that sundress." Bruno handed me a beignet.

I looked down at the navel oranges dotting the dress. "This old thing?" I'd picked it up at a thrift store a month ago when we were traveling through Florida. The cotton was worn soft, but the print was still vibrant.

He nodded. "I'd like to peel it off you later."

"Peel—I get it. You think you're so funny." I took a bite of the beignet, moaning as I chewed the warm, sugary dough. "If I keep eating these babies, I'll have to get serious about exercising."

He watched me lick the powdered sugar off my fingertips. "I'll help you burn off calories later."

I giggled. "You're smitten."

He scoffed. "You think?"

"Hey, you two," Eugene said from behind us.

I turned, my eyes widening at the sight of the barred owl

perched on his shoulder still. The skunk, raccoons, squirrel, heron, and alligator were absent, though. "It looks like you lost your assistants."

"Yep, but it's for the best. None of them were potty trained. Poor Mr. Jingles kept threatening to spray the others when nature would call." He thumbed toward the owl. "This guy is sticking around, though. He appears to like the circus life."

"Don't we all," said a high-pitched voice behind Eugene.

I leaned to the side to see around the big bear shifter. "Hi, Gigi. How's Donatello doing this morning?"

She stepped up next to Eugene. Her lab coat was wrinkled with streaks of dirt. Her red hair had come loose from the knot on top of her head. "He's on the mend. He'll be up and moving later today, I'm sure."

"Thanks for the warning," Bruno said, taking a sip of coffee.

"Are you heading out then?" I asked, sorry to see her go.

"That depends," she said.

"On what?" Eugene's question had a depth of something more than mere curiosity.

She blinked her long red lashes up at him. "You."

"Me?"

"Donatello and Marco offered me a job here at the circus as a traveling veterinarian, but we agreed that I need to be part of an act to keep AC from squawking about taking on new crew members."

"An act?" Eugene's thick brows lowered.

"I was wondering if you still need an assistant to help light your matches."

The shifter's smile equaled his bear size. "I sure do."

"You mind letting me join your act?"

"Little lady, nothing would make me happier than having you on stage by my side."

Ahhhh. Eugene's wish had come true after all.

I stuffed another beignet in my mouth, chewing with happiness.

"Electra!"

I looked across the grass to find Hank striding toward me. "Howdy, Hank. Where's your big kitty?"

"Back in my tent."

"What?" My smile faltered. I'd thought with the Wish spell revoked, everything would return to normal. Well, as normal as a freakshow circus could be. "Is he still playing kitty with you?"

"No, but we both realized during this wish mixup that it's lonely living alone and we enjoy the same books, so he moved in. We're going to try being roommates for a while."

He stopped at the order window long enough to ask for a couple of coffees, and then he joined us. "I wanted to thank you."

"For what? You still have a big cat living with you."

His lower lip stuck out. "That's true, but he's not sleeping in my bed or sitting on my lap anymore."

"That's good to hear. I'm glad it worked out for you two."

The sound of an elephant trumpeting made Hank's ears perk up. "That's Geraldine. She's waiting for her breakfast. I'd better run." He hurried off, grabbing the coffees in the pickup window on his way to the elephants' tent.

"Donatello is looking for you two," Gigi said to Bruno and me, shifting her doctor's bag to her other hand.

"Did he ever tell you what he wished for that started this ordeal?" Bruno asked.

She nodded. "It was an accident. Those show bunnies of his wouldn't stop hopping around him and singing 'Camptown Races' while he was trying to train them. He got mad and wished they'd shut up and get in their trunk."

"You're kidding," I said, shaking my head. "Those cute bunnies were behind this whole calamity."

Bruno laughed. "Finn was right about them being troublemakers." He tugged on my elbow. "Let's go."

We weaved through the tents to the monkey brothers' place. Upon arriving, Marco led us inside to Donatello's kip.

"Electra and Bruno," Donatello said with a tired smile. "I'm glad you're here. I wanted to thank you again for your help."

I pointed at the candle and partially burned feather on his nightstand. "What are you going to do with those?"

"Burn them both and dump them down a well, like I was supposed to in the first place. You see, I'd started the spell process, but then was called away to check on the flamingo triplets. Apparently, some weremuskrats hooligans had been trying to ruffle the girls' feathers the night before. Anyway, when I got back, I'd forgotten about the spell and went on with my daily routine, which included training the bunnies."

"We heard how you ended up in the trunk," Bruno said.

Donatello shook his head. "That's what I get for being greedy. I wanted to use the Wish spell to increase our profits. AC might send more money our way for new tents and equipment if we show some good revenue growth. In the end, I almost got myself killed and endangered everyone else."

"Voodoo is not a religion to dabble in," I said.

"So I've learned the hard way."

"Why were you stuck in your shifter form?" Bruno asked.

"I sometimes shift when I'm panic-stricken. The wish must have pushed me over the edge." He leaned back into his pillows, covering a yawn. "I want you both to know that I'm going to listen to my brother from now on and try to increase our profits with marketing, not black magic and frugality."

"Thank God," Bruno said dryly.

I elbowed him. "What Bruno means is that all of us here at the circus will be happy to help increase revenues within our means."

"Excellent."

"He needs to rest," Marco said, holding back the curtain leading to the main room.

We said our good-byes for now and joined Marco, who followed us outside into the warm morning sunlight.

"Thanks again, you two. Without your help, this all would

have ended badly."

He shook Bruno's hand and then gave me a hug.

"Electra and I need to get to work," Bruno told Marco and led me away before I got teary-eyed again.

After a few seconds of letting him pull me along toward the edge of the line of tents, I asked, "Where are we going?"

"To the swamp."

"Why? Are you going to throw me to the alligators?"

"Maybe, but not in broad daylight."

At the fence line, he pulled out his keys and opened a narrow gate that had been padlocked shut. We walked another hundred feet or so, and then he sat on a fallen log at the swamp's edge. He patted a spot next to him on the moss-covered bark.

"It's buggy out here." I sat with a scowl, swatting at something that buzzed around my head. "Now what?"

"I need to talk to you."

"And that required dragging me out to the swamp?"

His solemn nod gave me pause.

"What is it, Bruno?"

"I stopped in at work this morning before meeting you for coffee." He frowned toward the green water and cypress trees. "You remember that I still have the bounty hunter's cell phone."

"Oh, no." I gripped his forearm, steadying myself as the blood rushed from my head. "What about it?"

"There's a boss."

"I thought she worked alone."

"Me, too. Turns out we were wrong." He covered my hand with his. "Someone is looking for her, expecting her to have checked in by now."

"Oh, damn," I whispered, blowing out a breath. "It's just a matter of time before they come looking for her."

He nodded. "That doesn't mean they'll be looking for anyone else. Clint was on their radar, not you."

"We don't know if she sent word about me or not, though."

"Right. Well, for the time being we go on same as usual,

keeping an eye out for anyone who looks like trouble."

The urge to run far away always hovered in the back of my mind, but I pushed it away yet again. Bruno was here, along with my friends. I was as safe at the circus as anywhere else. Safer even, with the help I had.

"There's something else," Bruno said.

"Oh, shit. What else?"

"It's not as serious as the other problem," he added. "At least I don't think so."

"Tell me."

"I've been thinking about that wish you made to nullify the Wish spell." He glanced at me, his forehead lined. "I'm not sure it worked. At least not fully."

"What are you talking about? Donatello is back to his human form and talking."

"True, but he's different. Softer hearted. Not so black and white."

"He's learned his lesson."

He shrugged. "Maybe. But consider Eugene's wish."

"What about it? The animals are gone, except for the owl."

"Yes, but Gigi is going to be his assistant now, so his wish came true."

"Sort of," I said.

"Exactly. It came true, *sort of.* And don't forget Hank and Leon. They're now roommates. Before that wish Hank made, they barely spoke to each other."

"They've become good friends through this crisis. That's a good thing."

"Sure."

I sat next to him looking out at the swamp, letting his theory sink in. "What about you?" I asked. "You aren't overanalyzing everything anymore."

"That's mostly true, but think about us and last night in bed."

"What about it?" I smiled at him. We'd connected on a new level that felt deeper than a mere physical joining. "Sex was better than ever."

He looked my way, his eyes slightly narrowed. "Yeah …"

That word hung in the air between us like a swarm of gnats.

My eyes widened. "Oh! I see."

He nodded. "Everyone who made a wish has had their lives shift slightly in one way or another."

I chewed on my lower lip. "Gigi closed down the spell."

"Yep. So however we all ended, this is where we're stuck."

I took his hand in mine. "Do you want to talk about how that makes you feel?"

He laughed and pulled me to my feet. "No, but if I start writing you love sonnets, woman, you'd better pretend to like them."

I smiled up at him. "If you ask nicely, Eugene will let you read his romance books for inspiration."

"Oh, hell." He groaned. "This mushy mumbo-jumbo is going to be the end of me yet."

I giggled. "You have such a way with words, Romeo."

The End … for now

About the Author

Ann Charles is a *USA Today* bestselling author who writes award-winning mysteries that are splashed with humor, romance, paranormal elements, and whatever else she feels like throwing into the mix. When she is not dabbling in fiction, arm-wrestling with her children, attempting to seduce her husband, or arguing with her sassy cats, she is daydreaming of lounging poolside at a fancy resort with a blended margarita in one hand and a great book in the other.

Facebook (Personal Page):
http://www.facebook.com/ann.charles.author

Facebook (Author Page):
http://www.facebook.com/pages/Ann-Charles/37302789804?ref=share

Twitter (as Ann W. Charles):
http://twitter.com/AnnWCharles

Ann Charles Website:
http://www.anncharles.com

Books in the Deadwood Mystery Series

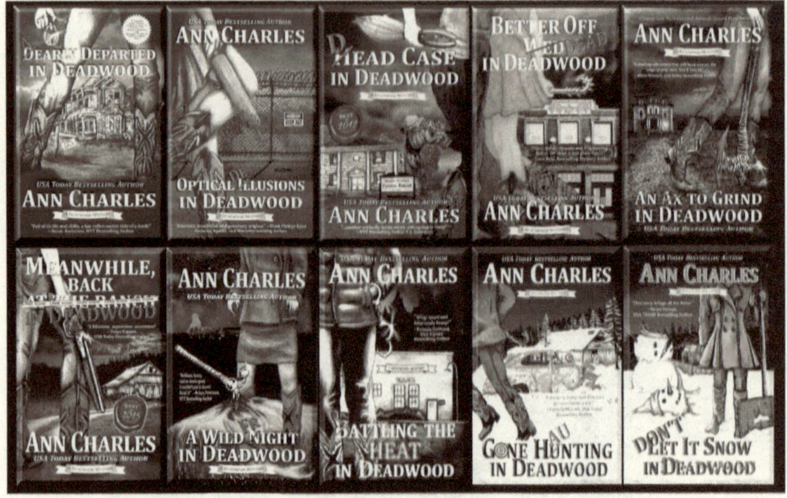

WINNER of the 2010 Daphne du Maurier Award for Excellence in Mystery/Suspense

WINNER of the 2011 Romance Writers of America® Golden Heart Award for Best Novel with Strong Romantic Elements

Welcome to Deadwood—the Ann Charles version. The world I have created is a blend of present day and past, of fiction and non-fiction. What's real and what isn't is for you to determine as the series develops, the characters evolve, and I write the stories line by line. I will tell you one thing about the series—it's going to run on for quite a while, and Violet Parker will have to hang on and persevere through the crazy adventures I have planned for her. Poor, poor Violet. It's a good thing she has a lot of gumption to keep her going!

Short Stories from Ann's
Deadwood Mystery Series

The Deadwood Shorts collection includes short stories featuring the characters of the Deadwood Mystery series. Each tale not only explains more of Violet's history, but also gives a little history of the other characters you know and love from the series. Rather than filling the main novels in the series with these short side stories, I've put them into a growing Deadwood Shorts collection for more reading fun.

The Goldwash Mystery Series

A sizzling, suspenseful SHORT STORY wrapped in a puzzling mystery that will leave you hungry for more.

It's "Groundhog Day" meets the modern day Old West!

In the lonely mining ghost town of Goldwash, Nevada, Christmas has come early. Unfortunately, the local bar owner must be on this year's naughty list, because Santa brought her something even worse than a piece of coal on this dark, cold winter night—her old man.

The Jackrabbit Junction Mystery Series

Bestseller in Women Sleuth Mystery and Romantic Suspense

Welcome to the Dancing Winnebagos RV Park. Down here in Jackrabbit Junction, Arizona, Claire Morgan and her rabble-rousing sisters are really good at getting into trouble—BIG trouble (the land your butt in jail kind of trouble). This rowdy, laugh-aloud mystery series is packed with action, suspense, adventure, and relationship snafus. Full of colorful characters and twisted up plots, the stories of the Morgan sisters will keep you wondering what kind of a screwball mess they are going to land in next.

The Dig Site Mystery Series

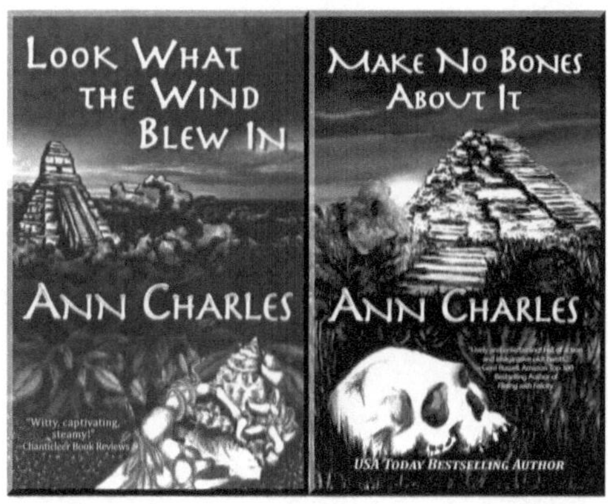

Welcome to the jungle—the steamy Maya jungle that is, filled with ancient ruins, deadly secrets, and quirky characters. Quint Parker, renowned photojournalist (and lousy amateur detective), is in for a whirlwind of adventure and suspense as he and archaeologist Dr. Angélica García get tangled up in mysteries from the past and present in exotic dig sites. Loaded with action and laughs, along with all sorts of steamy heat, these two will keep you sweating along with them as they do their best to make it out of the jungle alive in every book.